I, PEARL HART

I, PEARL HART

A Western Story

Jane Candia Coleman

Five Star
Unity, Maine

Five Star Western
Published in conjunction with Golden West Literary Agency.

February 1998

First Edition, second printing.

Five Star Standard Print Western Series.

The text of this edition is unabridged.

Set in 11 pt. Plantin by Al Chase.

Printed in the United States on permanent paper.

Library of Congress Cataloging in Publication Data

Coleman, Jane Candia.
    I, Pearl Hart : a western story / by Jane Candia Coleman.
— 1st ed.
      p. cm.
    ISBN 0-7862-0987-9 (hc : alk. paper)
    1. Hart, Pearl — Fiction. 2. Women outlaws — West (U.S.)
— Fiction.   I. Title.
    PS3553.O47427I3 1998
    813′.54—dc21
                                        97-38394

ACKNOWLEDGMENTS

My sincere thanks to my husband, Glenn Boyer, who cheerfully accompanied me on research trips and read and re-read this manuscript without complaint; to Jim and Aline Bywater and Larry Kellner for their invaluable insights; to Joan and John Freytag, who introduced me to Yuma prison and helped me in my search for documents; to the Yuma Prison Archives and the Arizona Historical Society; to Linda Hunt Ortega, who ignited my curiosity; to my neighbor, Tony Celaya, who helped me with Spanish not found in the dictionary; to Ben Traywick, Tombstone historian; and to editor, Jon Tuska, who believed in me and in this book. Bless you all!

Prologue

ARIZONA DAILY STAR

June 1, 1899

We have a woman bandit. Stage held up by a man and a woman. They secured three hundred and fifty dollars, a six shooter, and a gold watch from the passengers.

ASSOCIATED PRESS

Phoenix, May 31, 1899

Arizona has a woman bandit. She helped a male companion to hold up the Globe and Florence stage yesterday. Neither of the robbers wore a mask, and though the smaller wore men's clothing, there was no doubt of her sex.

Chapter One

Chicago, 1893

The pain from my cracked ribs snaked around, coiled, struck again and again until it was all I could do not to scream. I was lying half in and half out of an empty freight car, waiting for the pain to recede so I could pull myself in, find a dark corner where I could take care of my wounds, and where Frank couldn't find me.

Frank! I choked at the thought of him — his hands, passionate one minute, brutal the next, the thud of his polished boots against my body. I choked, and blood streamed out of my nose — it, too, was probably broken. I prayed I hadn't left a trail, like bright red flowers for him to follow. But no, he'd been passed out drunk after he'd beaten me, battered his ugly way into me.

I should have killed him, taken the big kitchen knife, and stabbed and stabbed, but to murder required strength, and I had only enough to save myself, wrapping my ribs in a strip of blanket and then, with the cunning of the soon-to-be hunted, dressing in Frank's old clothes. With the knife I hacked off my hair, that dark rope that had reached to my waist. In minutes I became a boy, a youth in search of adventure.

Who, looking for Pearl, would bother with a skinny runaway? I took the knife and the money I'd earned singing for Dan Sandeman, packed a loaf of bread and some tins of tomatoes and sardines in a sack, plus what was left of the precious laudanum I'd come to depend on. That would have to do. If I died of starvation, or cold, or loneliness somewhere out on the western prairie, well, at least I'd be free with no one to answer to, no hands to snap my bones like twigs.

I didn't run. It was all I could do to walk toward the station yard, bent over against the pain, against the damned wind off the lake that struck through my clothes. I kept going, wiping my bleeding nose on my sleeve and promising myself, if I got out of Chicago, I'd never be cold again, never let a man lay hands on me again, not if I lived a hundred years.

I circled around the station house and into the train yard. Somewhere ahead an engine breathed in and out, like the sound of my heart. Stumbling across the tracks, I saw the car looming ahead, its door open, and I summoned what strength was left to crawl in, hoping I'd not done more damage to myself.

As it was, I nearly fainted, but after a moment I dragged myself into a corner. Then the voice came out of nowhere.

"What're you doing in here?"

I couldn't speak over my fright. When I did, my voice came out cracked, like a kid's. "Going West," I said, and waited, straining my eyes, my ears, to locate the speaker in the darkness.

"This car's taken." No willingness to share in those words.

"Can't leave. My ribs are busted."

A rustle as the speaker came closer. "On the lam?"

I shook my head, then realized I was invisible. "Nope." I thought fast with the accuracy of desperation. "My stepfather beat me. I'm getting out before he kills me."

Another rustle. I could feel the warmth of a body, smell stale breath.

"Got any food?"

"Bread. Tomatoes and sardines." Best not to mention the money — or the knife. I put my hand in my pocket and touched the cold steel. "You're welcome to some," I said, and prayed. If he saw through my disguise, came at me, touched me, I'd use it on him.

"What's your name, kid?"

10

"Pete," I said. "What's yours?"

"Joe. Where you hiding those tomatoes?"

I reached into my sack and found the can, held it out, and jumped when a powerful hand caught my wrist.

"Damn' puny. How old are you?"

"Nineteen," I lied, and tried to pull away. This was almost worse than Frank's beatings. At least there I knew what the end would be, who my attacker was.

"Get your hand off me," I said.

Surprisingly he did, taking the can with him. "Just trying to see in the dark," he explained. "When we get moving, I got a lantern I can light. For now, we got to stay quiet and out of sight, or those railroad dicks'll throw us out. Maybe bust a few more ribs."

I let out my breath and felt the stab in my side. "Just leave me alone."

He scuffled around. Shortly I felt the tickle of straw. "Lots of this in here," he said. "Keeps you warm. You'll need it when we start moving and that wind cuts through the cracks. I'm shutting the door now. It'll be as dark as the inside of Jonah's whale."

"I don't care."

I didn't, either. I wanted to sleep and figured, if he came too close, I'd wake up and do whatever I had to do.

"Good thing." He got up, and I saw him silhouetted against the night sky — gaunt as a scarecrow, but strong, with dark whiskers.

"What are *you* doing in here?" I asked.

He turned. "Mind your own business."

The whites of his eyes flickered before he shut the door, and we were closed in together.

The train shuddered down its length, rocked, backed up, then began to move, and in that moment I knew I was safe,

11

that I'd get wherever it was I was going, and that Frank wouldn't find me.

The whistle blew. It sounded like a scream, like the sound of my past — the tears, the wounds, my own foolishness. For better or worse, I was on my way.

Even with a swallow of laudanum it was a bad night. The rocking of the train slammed my ribs, and Joe's dim lantern light quivered through the dusty car and shone on my face.

He ate half the tomatoes, using his fingers, then drinking the juice that stained his beard red. He wiped his mouth on his sleeve, then held out the can.

"Here, kid. Best eat something. A good wind'll blow you away."

I didn't want to eat or put my mouth where his had been, but hunger won. I emptied the can and put it down. He was watching me.

"Something wrong?" I asked, trying my best to sound tough.

"You ain't no beauty. Not with those black eyes."

Startled, I put my hands to my face.

He nodded. "Busted your nose, I reckon. Big fella, was he?"

"I couldn't lick him."

"Huh." He stretched out, propping his head in his hand. "Nobody's licked me since I was twelve. I been on my own ever since. Seen lots of country."

In spite of my pain, I was interested. "What do you do?"

"Anything that needs doing. I'm headed for the mines. Hard work, but I figure sooner or later I'll get lucky."

"What kind of mines? Where?"

"Arizona Territory. Lots of mines . . . copper, silver, gold. They say up in Globe they found a piece of silver so big it weighed damn' near a ton. Called it Munson's Chunk after

12

the guy who found it. Must be there's more where that came from, and, besides, it's warm. Not like this damned country. Turn you to stone, that wind out there, and that's a fact."

"How do you get there? To Arizona?"

"Find a train headed that way."

"Are we on one?"

I hoped we were. Oh, I hoped! His answer dashed that.

"Nope. Got to hop another in K. C."

I wrapped my arms around myself to steady my aching ribs. "Can I go with you?"

"I travel alone," he said. "Can't be nursemaidin' young 'uns."

"I can cook."

He grinned. "You see a stove in here?"

It was a ridiculous notion. I'd known it from the start. "Never mind," I said. "I'll get there by myself." I closed my eyes and huddled into the straw.

I thought I would sleep, but scenes from the past kept chasing themselves across the darkness behind my eyes.

Chapter Two

Toledo, 1886

I fastened my new skates and took off across the pond, leaving my friends clustered like ducks on the bank.

Oh, it was glorious — the speed, the freedom of motion, the very daring of it all! Not for me the rôle of helpless female, waiting breathlessly for the support of a masculine arm. At sixteen, I was headstrong, sure of myself, impatient with the do's and don't's of what was termed "proper behavior."

Faster I went, and faster, my laughter trailing behind me. "Catch me if you can!"

Suddenly I wasn't alone. Another skater appeared, matching me stride for stride. I had a quick glimpse of his face — white teeth, a wildness in his eyes that echoed my own. A race! I'd show him! I knew the course, and it was dangerous — through the swamp toward the Maumee River. Tussocks of grass were trapped in the ice, and the trunks of dead trees laid their snares just below the surface.

In the light of the setting sun the ice glimmered, a sheet of gold. I sped across it, and the stranger followed, accepting my challenge. He was good. Better than good. None of the boys I knew had ever kept up with me, those boys with their sweaty hands and breath like warm milk. I shuddered at the thought and went faster.

Who was this man who moved so effortlessly, his scarf a streak of crimson against the darkening sky?

My lungs were burning. Never before had I skated so far and at such a pace. A quick glance showed my challenger, keeping pace easily with what seemed to be a sneer on his lips. Was he laughing at me? Furious, I pushed on, but emotion was my undoing. My toe caught a branch hidden under the ice, and I fell headlong, sprawling ungracefully and with a nasty pain in my ankle.

He knelt beside me, and in spite of pain and anger I was aware of the heat of his hands on my waist. "Are you all right? That was a bad fall." His face was close to mine, his eyes gleaming like opals.

If I had ever been one to follow the rules, I would have fainted then and there in the manner of a properly brought up young lady. But I was mad all the way through, at myself and at him for making me look foolish.

"Damn you!" I exclaimed. "It's all your fault."

He threw back his head and laughed, and my heart turned over.

"Who are you?" I asked, struggling to sit up.

"Frank Hart. Your friend Lizzie's cousin. The black sheep of the family."

"Oh." I studied him in the gathering darkness. Everybody in Toledo knew about Frank Hart. How he'd run away from school and gone West to make his fortune, and how he'd made it gambling and in other ways that were never mentioned, merely hinted at with raised brows and much whispering.

"I see you've heard about me."

He was grinning like a tomcat, and suddenly I smiled back. Black sheep or not, he was a better bargain than any of the boys I knew. And, besides, I enjoyed the way his hand lingered on my waist.

"If my mother knew you were coming to skate, she'd have locked me in the closet," I said.

"That bad?"

"Worse."

"Pity."

"Why?"

"Because I was intending to call on you."

I pictured it — my mother's shock, and the scolding that was sure to follow. On the spur of the moment I said: "You may call on me, Mister Hart. That is, if I can make it home on this ankle."

"I'll carry you," he said gallantly. "I've never abandoned a lady in distress."

For a few moments we stared at each other, and I thought he was going to kiss me, *wished* for it, though I'd never been kissed and had only a schoolgirl's knowledge of what went on between men and women gained from reading forbidden romance novels.

"Pearl! Pearl! Where are you?" The shouts of the others broke the spell, and the sound of my name seemed like the cry of the wind or the lonely keening of gulls over the harbor.

"The name suits you," he whispered.

I swallowed my disappointment over the kiss and said nothing, but he read my face. Taking off one glove, he reached out and gently stroked my cheek.

"Later," he said.

It sounded like a promise.

Chapter Three

"It's unseemly. Letting that man bring you home! I brought you up better than this. You're a lady, not a boy, and you don't know where men like that will lead you."

I didn't, of course. But I wished I could find out.

It was two days later, and my mother was scolding. I was in the front room, restless and beside myself, my ankle propped up on an ottoman. My Christmas vacation from school was ruined. I was trapped and helpless, and I'd probably never get to see Frank again in spite of my invitation to call. Tears of frustration ran down my cheeks.

"You should cry," my mother went on. "Maybe you'll remember your upbringing next time."

Her words meant nothing to me. I'd been hearing them since I could remember, and they were always the same. *You'll disgrace us all! No man will have you!*

Perhaps in her eyes I had unsexed myself, but what I'd felt there on the ice had been simply my own wanting, the first clue as to what womanhood was about. My mother made me feel like the ugly duckling, hatched in the wrong nest. When I wanted to fly, which was all the time, I found my wings clipped. I hid my face in my handkerchief and cried harder.

And then someone knocked on the door.

"Stop crying," my mother snapped, in a complete reversal of mood. "You'll ruin your appearance."

Obediently, I mopped my tears. I wished it would be Frank at the door, but any company at all would be a welcome distraction.

Lizzie O'Riley came in with a flurry of skirts and knelt beside my chair. "How do you feel? Does it hurt terribly? We've all come to cheer you up." She lowered her voice to a whisper. "Frank's here, too. He didn't think your mother would let him in by himself, so we all came. Teddy, Violet, Oscar, and me."

"He's here?" My heart leaped into my throat. And then I saw him, still wearing that scarlet muffler and looking more handsome in the day than he had in the shadows of twilight.

He dropped a bouquet of crimson carnations in my lap.

"For me?" My voice came out in a whisper.

"Who else?" He stood there, black-haired and smiling and completely at ease.

No one had ever given me flowers. I was a schoolgirl still, at that age between childhood and womanhood. But at that moment I crossed an invisible line. Pearl Taylor burst out of her shell and became a woman with all of a woman's passion.

The carnations seemed to burn my hands with their flaming beauty. I caressed the petals, inhaled the spicy scent, and searched for words to give meaning to my feelings.

My mother's horror at seeing Frank was overcome by her thrifty nature. "I'll put these in a vase," she said, and headed toward the kitchen.

"Thank you," I said when she was gone. "I wish I could keep them forever."

"You're more beautiful than any flower," he said, leaning down and taking my hand. "You know that?"

Struck dumb, I shook my head.

"You will." He stared at my mouth with those wild eyes of his, as if he couldn't get enough of looking. "I'll keep telling you until you believe it."

I wanted to touch him. I wanted him to touch me, so that it would be his hands that burned, not the petals of flowers. All I wanted was to be alone with him.

18

Of course, he knew what he was doing, knew his effect on women. I couldn't know then that, behind the silken words, the promises, the wonder of it all, was a man unsure of himself, a human without respect or caring for others, one to whom women were simply objects to be used and discarded like broken toys. At sixteen I was restless, tired of the rules and wrappings of middle-class society. In short, I was an easy mark.

Chapter Four

I was born in Ontario, Canada. My father, James Taylor, was a civil engineer who moved his family to Toledo in 1878 when I was seven, in the hope of finding a better job. This he did, but his work kept him away from home and left my mother to deal with the household and the raising of two daughters. My sister, Maude, was quiet and biddable from the first. Uprooted, torn away from the security of my childhood home, I let out my misery like the little savage I was, always running away to the docks and the train station in futile attempts to go back to the past.

I hated the new house, the Catholic school that Maude and I attended, the rules and regulations. I missed my dog, Duke, whom we'd left behind, detested the scrawny kittens Maude kept bringing home to take his place. Some day, I vowed to myself, I'd be free, grown up, and could go where I wanted, act as I pleased.

In desperation, my parents sent me to boarding school in Cleveland where they hoped the nuns would achieve what they couldn't. To an extent, the nuns succeeded. At least in appearance, I was a lady with proper manners and the ability to converse politely. Though I wore these habits lightly, like a cloak I could take off at will, my parents, on the whole, were satisfied. I wasn't. Nor was I enchanted at the idea of going back once Christmas vacation was over.

Locked up in the convent, I'd never see Frank again. The very thought was agony. At night, sleepless, I imagined a thousand scenes in which I escaped and was welcomed into his arms with tender passion.

Oh, he'd been clever! In the week following my accident he came with all my friends to the house. Often by three in the afternoon ten or more of us would be in our parlor, laughing, talking, playing the silly games that were in vogue, and even dancing. Although I was unable to dance, I played the piano and led the singing. Music was my one pleasure. I let out my feelings in song, taking comfort in the thought that no one could recognize them.

"You're very good." Frank stood beside me, turning the pages.

I blushed and stumbled over a piece I'd perfected several years before.

"Tell me something," he went on, perfectly aware that he could not be heard by anyone but me. "What in hell are you doing here? You don't belong with these children. Look at them!" He gestured at the room, then turned back to me. "Singing away like a bunch of baby birds in a nest and pretending to have fun."

"Maybe they are," I murmured.

"Ha! I could show you fun. Places like you've never dreamed, music like you've never heard before. Don't tell me you enjoy this . . . this kindergarten."

What I enjoyed was having him beside me, showering compliments, telling me that I didn't belong. That I was destined for better things than parlor games, marriage to a dull husband, and the motherhood that mysteriously seemed to follow.

"I don't know how to answer you," I said.

He laughed and bent close, so close I could feel his breath. "With the truth," he whispered. "You don't have to lie to me. I know you. I knew you the minute I saw you, skating away like the devil was after you."

I smiled. "Maybe he was."

"And maybe you wanted it," he countered.

Once again my fingers tangled over a chord. "Please."

"I don't please. I'm telling you what you ought to know. You're different. You don't belong here with these biddies."

"And where should I be, Mister Hart?"

"Waltzing with kings," came the response. "In a red velvet gown with rubies in your hair and a gardenia between those pretty breasts."

I should have been shocked. I should have gotten up then and there and never spoken to him again. But the picture he'd painted was so close to those I'd dreamed that I stayed and kept on playing though my heart beat so fast I was sure he could see it, fluttering under my bodice.

"I do hate it here," I muttered. What I meant was that I wished he'd take me away. Anywhere.

"Of course, you do," he said. "Lovely Pearl."

The song I was playing came to an end, but suddenly he began another, unaccompanied. "Beautiful dreamer. . . . awake unto me. . . ."

Listening to his sweet tenor voice, seeing how his eyes gleamed when he looked at me, I knew that I loved him with all my heart.

Chapter Five

We were packing my trunk for my return to school when my mother suddenly sank down on the bed. Although her face was flushed, she was shivering.

"What is it?" I was frightened for, in spite of her limited views on life, I cared for her — more than I was able to admit.

"I'm coming down with something," she whispered, her voice a croak.

I hobbled on my still-weakened ankle to the top of the stairs and called for Annie, the maid. Together we got my mother into bed, then Annie motioned me out into the hall.

"You best plan on stayin' home a while," she told me. " 'Least till that fever breaks."

"Of course," I said.

Later, sitting beside my mother's bed, I realized that her illness was a reprieve and perhaps a blessing in disguise. Always in the past she had gone with me on the train to school, suspecting that I'd somehow disgrace myself or attempt to run away. Now what I had to do was convince her that I was grown up enough to travel alone.

I thought of freedom, and of Frank. The two words were like wine, making me giddy. When, later that afternoon, the knock came on the door, I was breathless with excitement. Surely, alone with him, something would happen, at the very least that promise of a kiss.

"Mother's sick!" I announced as Frank and Lizzie came in.

As usual, Lizzie was quick. "Would she like some company?"

"You could see if she needs anything," I told her. "I still can't go up and down stairs too well."

Frank followed me into the parlor. "What game shall we play now that we're alone?" he asked, smiling wickedly.

I looked up at him, trying to gauge his intentions and perceiving they were the same as mine. Still, all that early training, the voices of the nuns, intervened. *Never show a man you're interested! Keep yourself pure. Men don't marry tarnished goods!* I hesitated. Was a kiss enough to tarnish me forever? I decided to find out.

"Whatever you choose," I said, and blushed much to my disgust.

He laughed at that and raised an eyebrow. I thought he looked like a pirate or the hero of one of my romance novels.

"Will you sing for me?"

That was the last thing I wanted, singing songs about love instead of doing something about it.

"If you want." Purposely I sounded ungracious.

He laughed again, and I wondered if he was teasing me and, if so, what I should do about it.

"Ah, Pearl," he said at last. "Don't you know what I want? And don't you think I've heard all the old ladies' advice? And do you think for a minute I give a damn about any of it?"

I stared at him. "You don't?"

"No. And neither should you. They only want to keep you from having fun."

Since he was saying exactly what I thought, I said: "They treat me like I'm a baby, and I'm not."

The glint went out of his eyes and was replaced by a darkness I couldn't read. "No," he said. "You're not. You're only asleep, like the princess in the fairy tale. Like the poet wrote once."

"Poetry," I said scornfully, dreading the moment when he'd

start reciting some saccharine rhyme of the type that I'd been forced to memorize, when all I wanted was to be kissed.

"Not the kind you're thinking about." He put his hands on my shoulders and drew me close, so close I could feel his breath on my face. "'Asleep or waking is it?'" he murmured. "'For her neck, kissed over close, wears yet a purple speck wherein the pained blood falters and goes out; soft and stung softly, fairer for a fleck.'" And then he bent his head and found my lips.

I should have been shocked, shamed by the insistence of his tongue against mine, by the way his hands slid down to my hips and stayed there, but instead I was swept by a longing so huge I put my arms around his neck and pressed my body into his.

How long did it last? Long enough to prove that my dreams were more than the stifled imaginings of a child.

"For God's sake!" Frank pulled away. "Not here! Not now!"

But I had felt him throbbing against me with an insistence equal to my own, and I didn't give up easily.

"Where? When?"

His eyes shown with that wolfish wildness I'd been attracted to from the first and with something that I now realize was recklessness, for Frank was, above all, reckless, living for the moment, uncaring about past or future. "Don't go back to school. Come away with me. You'll be dancing in your red dress before the month is out, and that's a promise, darlin'."

It seemed that all the pieces of an impossible puzzle fell into place with his words. I'd pretend to leave for school, but instead I'd run away with Frank Hart.

"Yes," I whispered. "Yes, yes, yes!"

He caught me up again and whispered into my hair. "We'll go to New Orleans. By boat, if the river's not iced up. Ah, darlin', what a time we'll have!"

It was happening! Elated, I held onto him, blinking back tears of joy. Little did I know how soon those tears would turn to tears of heartbreak. His next words should have warned me.

"I'll meet you at the station. We'll go from there to Cincinnati. And bring all the money you can get your hands on."

"Money!" I exclaimed, shocked. "Why do I need money?"

He kissed me again — on my eyelids, the tip of my nose. "Because, darlin', I'm a gambler, and I like to keep a stash."

Chapter Six

Frank Hart and I were married a week later by Captain Robert Lassiter in his quarters on board the steamboat, *The Golden Rule*. The wedding night had come before the ceremony in the hotel where we registered as Mr. and Mrs. Frank Hart.

A woman never forgets her awakening to love and passion, even when it turns to ashes, and Frank, with experienced fingers, with lips and tongue and murmured words, initiated me into the pleasures that can exist between a man and a woman.

Time and time again he brought me to the point where nothing would satisfy but his maleness. Time and time again I screamed his name, not caring if anyone heard. In fact, I was beyond caring about anything other than what I felt.

"You're famous, darlin'!" Frank tossed a copy of *The Golden Rule*'s newspaper onto the bed.

Mr. Frank Hart and Miss Pearl Taylor were married on board yesterday by Captain Lassiter. Mr. Hart is well known to us. The lovely bride is on her first trip to New Orleans.

"My mother always said that a woman's name should appear only when she was born, when she got married, and when she died," I said, smoothing the paper with one finger.

"What she knows, you could fit in a thimble." He climbed

in beside me. "Who knows how many times your name'll be in the paper?"

"Or for what?" I added, shivering a little.

"Cold?" His arm tightened around me. "We'll soon fix that."

"A goose on my grave," I said, laughing, unable to explain the feeling of dread that had come out of nowhere.

"An old wives' tale." He buried his face in my breasts. "I personally prefer young wives' tails."

"Naughty," I teased.

"And you love it."

"I love you," I said, and succumbed to bliss.

But even before our trip was over, I had a glimpse of the dark side of Frank's character.

The salon of *The Golden Rule* had been cleared of tables and chairs for an evening dance. All the first-class passengers were there, and at first I was shy for I had only one gown and *that quite out of place* I thought as I watched the women waltzing — their jewels glittering on bare shoulders and bosoms, their gowns of lace and tulle, flowers and ribbons putting me in the shade.

"May I have the pleasure of this dance, Missus Hart?" Frank bowed in front of me, and, smiling, I gave him my hand.

I loved dancing, and Frank was an excellent partner. We waltzed until I was hot and breathless.

"Goodness! I haven't ever had so much fun," I said, as he danced me off the floor to a row of chairs against the wall. The older women sat there, fanning themselves and gossiping and keeping a close eye on their young daughters who watched the dancing with a longing I quite understood. Only a few weeks before I had been one of them.

"I promise you'll have more fun when we get to New

Orleans and you've got your red dress," Frank said.

He hadn't forgotten! I wanted to throw my arms around him in gratitude, but the old dowagers were watching, and some restrictions of the past still controlled my actions.

"I can't wait!" I said, trying to get my breath, always difficult with corset stays digging into me.

"Sit down and rest a minute," Frank said. "There's a man I want to see. And I'm sure Missus Chambers will be glad of your company." He smiled at the lady next to me, who had taken a fancy to us earlier and who beamed up at him. All the old ladies loved Frank, knowing nothing of his reputation, only that he was young, handsome, and newly married, and that he flirted with them as if they were belles.

"Your Pearl is safe with me, Mister Hart," she said, and patted my hand with her withered old one. "Such a lovely bride."

"She is, indeed," he said, and bowed to her which caused her to fan herself more violently.

"And such a lovely husband," she murmured to me when he'd gone. "I remember when I was first married. . . ."

She began a long reminiscence I hardly listened to. I was watching the dancers and growing restless. I wanted to join them, to be moving in time to the music — the reels, schottisches, waltzes that I loved. And Frank had been gone a long time.

My desire must have showed in my face — or in my feet that were keeping time beneath my skirt. And a man who had been standing by the piano met my eyes and understood.

The next minute he was in front of me. "May I have the pleasure of this dance?"

What to do? I looked for permission to Mrs. Chambers, who was smiling. "Go, my dear," she urged. "And if your husband returns, I'll tell him he shouldn't have kept you waiting so long."

Then I was waltzing again, happily, and my partner was smiling down at me.

"My name is Julian Plummer," he said. "And you wanted to dance so badly I decided to rescue you."

"I'm Missus Pearl Hart."

"Our new bride."

I nodded.

"How is it that you were sitting there alone?" he wanted to know.

"My husband had some business to attend to." I answered him firmly for it seemed he was criticizing Frank.

But all he said was, "I see," and swept me in a circle.

"You're a fine dancer."

"No finer than my partner."

It was polite conversation, no more, no less, but Frank, returning to the salon, misunderstood and cut in on us. He was angry. His eyes glittered, and his hand on my waist was cruel.

"Must I watch you every second now that I've gotten you out of the coop?" he demanded. "Keep you locked up, so you don't go running after every man you see?"

Shocked, I stared at him. "It was only one dance," I said. "And he . . . he was quite polite. Missus Chambers said. . . ."

"That old bat." His fingers tightened around my wrist, and I flinched.

"You're hurting me."

"So you'll remember you're my wife and act like it next time."

He shifted his grip to my shoulders and stopped dancing. I'd have bruises in the morning, marks put on me by my husband.

"Please!" I whispered, afraid to make a scene.

"Stop whining. I hate women who whine."

30

He was so different from the Frank I thought I knew that I searched his face, trying to find an answer. What I saw, frightened me. I saw a stranger with thin lips and unreadable eyes, a man possessed by something I couldn't name. Around us the dancers danced, the music went on, and no one seemed to notice my terror except for Julian Plummer who was once again leaning against the piano and watching us, one eyebrow raised at a slant.

"Let's go back to the room," I said.

Frank shook his head. "No, my dear. We're going to dance every dance. That's what you wanted. That's what you'll have."

He was as good as his word. While I danced, on sore feet and aching ankles, while my stays bit into me like knives and stole my breath, I remembered the story my mother used to read to me — about a girl who couldn't stop dancing, who died from what had begun as a pleasure. It was a story that she always ended with the admonishment to be moderate and modest in all things. And, as my pleasure turned into pain, I pleaded. "Can we stop? Can we please?" But my husband, the man I adored, kept me dancing until the music ended and all the lights went out.

In the morning he was apologetic, kissing my bruises as if to make them disappear. "You're as fragile as a flower," he whispered. "I couldn't stand seeing you with him. Forgive me?"

Could I? And could I forgive the way he had then thrown me on the bed and taken me, without tenderness or any seeming love at all?

"I mean it, darlin'. I guess . . . I guess I was just jealous. I never had a wife before."

And no one had ever been jealous on my account. I looked long into those greenish eyes of his and saw them filled with remorse. And I forgave him. By the time we docked in New Orleans, I had almost forgotten.

★ ★ ★ ★ ★

New Orleans, that lovely old city on the Delta, existed, or so it seemed to me, simply for pleasure. Although the days of Creole splendor were gone, remnants remained — the houses in the French Quarter still painted pink, yellow, blue, each with a secret, flower-scented courtyard, each protected by balconies of delicate wrought iron; the French market where anything could be bought or sold, as I would learn to my sorrow; the spicy Creole and Cajun food that I came to love; and the music, above all the music that never stopped, a mixture of all the races that inhabited the Quarter, a tapestry woven by banjos and cornets, trombones, and pianos, and underneath it all the song of the river, a dark counterpoint.

"I can take you back," it murmured from behind the restraining levee. "Anytime I want, I can take you back."

I had never seen anything to equal the splendor of the St. Charles Hotel and gawked, like the adolescent I was, at the lobby with its columns and chandeliers, its marble floors and velvet settees, and at the men and women who came and went as if they were a part of the decor.

Nervous, I clung to Frank's arm. "It must be very expensive," I whispered.

He laughed. "I'm flush, darlin'. You must've brought me luck. Enjoy it while you can."

Being a gambler's wife was a risky position, dependent on the luck of the draw, the quirk of the moment, but how could I know that? I simply assumed that we were rich and would always live this way — as honored passengers, in fine hotels, dressed in clothes that were the height of fashion, for the next day Frank took me to a dressmaker, a wizened little woman who spoke an almost unintelligible *patois* but whose eye was that of a true genius.

"No pale color for you, madame," she announced, seeing

32

me fingering a length of delicate pink silk. "Red. Yellow like the chrysanthemums on the graves on All Saints'. And blue like the sea."

I didn't like the idea of looking like a decoration on a tomb, but, to my delight, within a few days I had my red silk gown, its underskirt trimmed with bands of Cluny lace, and a walking costume of a blue so pure I was reminded not of the sea but of an iris, its petals changing color in the sun, and a day dress of golden faille with a short, tight-fitting jacket and a parasol to match.

"Now I'll take you to dinner at Antoine's," Frank said. "Wear the blue."

Julian Plummer was at a table near the door. He was alone, and I gave him a quick smile as we passed.

"Shall we ask your friend to join us?" Frank asked when we were seated.

"No!" I answered quickly. "And he's not my friend."

"As you wish." He bent over his plate of oysters with relish. "Oysters are for love," he said, swallowing the first. "At least, that's what they say."

I was pushing mine around on the plate. "Why?"

"They make men virile and ladies passionate. I bet none of the nuns or old ladies told you that one."

I giggled. The idea of any women I knew discussing virility was ridiculous. "Is it true?"

He shrugged. "Who knows? Who knows how superstitions start? Eat up, and we'll see what happens later."

But the sight of Plummer had stolen my appetite. I managed several, then pushed the plate across to Frank. "You eat them," I said. "I guess . . . I guess I'm just too excited."

But by the time the next course arrived, a fish baked in heavy paper, steaming and fragrant with spices, my appetite had returned, I had forgotten Plummer, and ate with delight.

★ ★ ★ ★ ★

The evening was warm and the streets of the Quarter were filled with people — tourists, locals, black and white. From somewhere came the sound of a piano, accompanied by a banjo. Laughter drifted through open doors and windows like an echo.

"Is it always like this? So alive?" I asked, taking Frank's arm.

"It's almost Mardi Gras. But, yes. This town doesn't sleep much."

"Mardi Gras?"

"The big celebration before Lent. They have parades and masked balls and dancing in the streets. It's an old tradition."

"Will we go to a ball?" I was thinking of my red gown, and of the magnolia blossoms that were everywhere.

He laughed. "Hardly. Those balls are for the old society. By invitation only. Not for the likes of you and me."

His words sank in. Standing there on the crowded banquette, I understood with finality what I had done. I had traded respectability for glitter, moved outside the pale, and was as much an outcast as Frank. For one moment I felt lonely, afraid, like the child I still was, the girl who, lured by excitement, now had only a gambling man between her and disaster.

He was smiling at me as if he read my mind. "There's plenty of places to dance if that's what you want," he said.

"Right now I'd like to go back to the hotel."

He misunderstood my insecurity, and his smile flickered into passion. "I'm at your service, Missus Hart," he said.

34

Chapter Seven

It seemed that from that evening on we ran into Julian Plummer wherever we went — to lunch at Lake Ponchartrain, in the book store where I had gone to find something to read on the nights Frank was gambling, and at the race track. It was there that I spoke with him again, to my sorrow.

Frank had gone to place a bet on a horse that had caught my eye, when I turned and saw Plummer standing beside me.

He took off his hat and bowed. "Good afternoon, Missus Hart."

"Mister Plummer," I said through stiff lips, terrified that Frank would come rushing back and drag me away.

"A fine day for the races, isn't it?" He was looking at me closely out of eyes the color of stone.

I nodded, not wishing to prolong the conversation but curious about what he was doing in town. "Are you here on business, Mister Plummer?" I asked.

"Partly," he said. "I own a plantation above Natchez and get down here several times a year. But like you and your husband, I'm simply enjoying myself."

"At all the same places," I said.

"It seems so."

I glanced over my shoulder, watching for Frank, and Plummer caught the gesture. "Is anything the matter?" he wanted to know.

"Nothing."

But he was quick. "I realize that your husband objected to our dance that night," he said. "I hope . . . I hope I didn't make any trouble for you. That wasn't my intention."

Did he know? Surely not. He had watched while Frank danced me into exhaustion, but he couldn't know about the bruises or about how, later, Frank had thrown me on the bed and taken me in an act that was more like hatred than love.

I lowered my parasol so that it shadowed my face. "No, Mister Plummer. But I think it would be better if he didn't see us together."

"I understand." He took my hand and bowed over it. "Dancing with you was a real pleasure. Perhaps we will do it again some day."

"Perhaps."

I stepped past him then, moving in the direction Frank had gone, and soon saw him approaching.

"Let's go and find a good place to watch that nag you thought was so pretty," he said, glancing over my head. "I see your friend is here."

"Who?" I pretended innocence.

"You know who. Is he following us?" He gripped my arm, his fingers biting deep.

Without success I tried to squirm loose. "I don't know what you're talking about," I said, and heard myself, weak as a child. "Let's go watch the race."

"Tell me the truth." He bent down, his face close to mine. I could smell whiskey on his breath, and the cigars he loved. "Has he spoken to you? Approached you? And don't lie."

"I haven't spoken to a soul!" I said, and prayed my lie wouldn't be stamped on my forehead.

Abruptly he let go. "I won't put up with a wife who's a whore," he said. "Remember that."

A whore! I thought bitterly as I followed him through the crowd. Never was a woman less of a whore than I was. How could he think such a thing, let alone speak of it, and all because of an innocent waltz?

The horse that I had picked came in last, and we lost heavily all afternoon. Frank hardly spoke on the ride back to the hotel, and he was silent at supper, too. I was nervous, trembling by the time we finished eating. I couldn't read his face — it was the gambler's studied blank — and I ate only a little, unable to swallow around my apprehension.

Once in the room, he washed his face and smoothed his hair, then turned to me. "I'm going to a cock fight," he announced. "I won't be back until late. And I'm taking the key. That way at least I can be sure of you."

I couldn't believe my ears. "You're locking me in?"

He nodded, then came and took my face in his hands and kissed me, his tongue possessing my mouth as if he were leaving a brand. "Yes, darlin'," he said when he drew away. "I'm keeping you safe."

He went out, and I heard the key turn in the lock. *Safe,* I thought bitterly and with a hint of panic. *Safe from what?* Then I lay down on the bed and cried myself to sleep.

In the morning, over breakfast, Frank was silent, almost morose, and I did nothing to lighten his mood. A pall lay over me that refused to lift, and I drank my coffee and ate a powdered *beignet* without speaking. I was lost in my own misery when Frank finally spoke.

"Where's the money you brought?"

I was startled and spilled some coffee onto the white table-cloth. "What money?"

"From home. And don't tell me you didn't."

"Oh," I said, remembering with a kind of shame how I'd taken my mother's household money from the drawer in the kitchen and then rifled her purse for more. "It's in my valise."

"Get it. And then start packing."

37

"Packing," I repeated, knowing I was at his mercy and hating it. *Being a wife was worse than being a daughter*, I thought. *Your husband dictated, and you obeyed without question.*

"You didn't think we could afford to stay here forever, did you?" he asked with a sneer. "I lost damn' near everything yesterday and last night. Now we're moving, so start packing."

"Where are we going?" At least, he could tell me that. At least, I'd have the security of a destination.

"A boarding house on Royal Street. It's the best I could find, so don't start complaining."

"I wasn't."

He looked at me for the first time that morning, and his expression softened. "That's how it is when you're married to a gambling man, darlin'. Better get used to it. My luck'll change again."

I pushed back my chair and stood. "I hope so," I said, and left to pack. There really wasn't anything else to do.

Chapter Eight

Once the boarding house in the Quarter had been a mansion. Now it was crumbling into disrepair, its yellow paint splotched with water stains and fallen chunks of plaster, the green shutters sagging, the parquet floors scarred by boarders who had no knowledge or use for an earlier elegance.

Once Lily Rousseau had been a belle. Now she was a crone with hair dyed black and cheeks painted crimson, a specter who clutched at the past as she struggled to hold onto the house that contained only echoes.

Lily knew what Frank was as soon as she laid eyes on him. What she couldn't seem to grasp was the fact that we were actually married.

"You could do better," she told me over tea in the shaded courtyard where I often sat to escape the heat. She sipped from her cup that held mostly brandy. Lily, I had discovered, was a drunk.

I said: "But I love Frank."

"Love!" she snapped. "Love! What do you know about it? You're a baby. I could tell you plenty about love, but you wouldn't believe me. No . . . you wouldn't." She wagged a bony finger as I tried to protest. "But he's no good, that man of yours. I guess you know that."

I defended him as I thought I should, in spite of his cruelties that were becoming more and more frequent.

"He's my husband. I won't let you say these things."

She put down her cup with an unsteady hand. "Child," she said, "when you're as old as I am, you can say anything you

39

damn' well please. Remember that. I've seen it all. Men, women, passion, the plague, war, death. I'm a walking history book."

When I stood up to leave, having no wish to continue the conversation, she reached out and caught my arm. "Don't go off in a huff. And don't let that man run roughshod over you. That's all I meant, and it's good advice."

"You sound like my mother."

"Then your mother's a smart lady," came the response. "I'll bet she doesn't care for that husband of yours any more than my mother liked the man I chose." Again she waggled a finger at me. "Oh yes, I was young once, and pretty, too, and this town was paradise, not like now. And I married a man I thought I loved. I wouldn't listen. I was headstrong and sure of myself. And that man was a gambler. He'd bet on anything, and I couldn't stop him." She closed her eyes, and I thought she'd gone to sleep, but a second later she opened them again and stared at me.

"He lost everything," she resumed. "All but this house, which was mine and my family's. I kept it. Yes, I did. And I'll keep it till I die, you can count on it."

"And your husband?" I asked, curious.

"He shot himself." She shook with what seemed to be silent laughter. "Couldn't stand the disgrace he'd brought on, I suppose. I made it look like an accident, so he'd at least have a proper funeral. Nobody dared say anything. Except me. I said . . . good riddance. That's what happens when you pick the wrong man. In the end you're glad to be rid of him."

She shut her eyes again and leaned back in her chair. Under the wrinkles and the rouge I could see the fine bones of a face that had once been beautiful, been young and grasping at life, and I was frightened, seeing myself in old age, alone and filled with regrets.

40

I got up and walked slowly through the neglected courtyard, through ferns and tea olive, jasmine and roses, through air so moist, so perfumed, I felt slightly dizzy. The city had that effect, I thought. It surrounded you with promises, so many you couldn't choose. And in the end, it abandoned you, left you wondering what you'd done or not done, and perhaps not caring.

It was a city of pleasure and gambling — a paradise or a hell, depending on luck. And Frank was in his element, betting wildly on the horses, the cocks, the prize fights that were illegal but that drew huge crowds of eager onlookers. I knew about them because he told me. What I didn't know was how much money he was losing.

I listened to him and tried to understand his excitement. And failed. Cock fighting was men's business — animals killing each other in a flurry of blood and feathers. What did that slaughter have to do with me, with us?

That afternoon he came in and woke me by going through the closet, snatching my gowns from their hangers.

"What's happening?" I sat up, dazed and blinking.

"These go to the market. I need the money." He answered without feeling, as if I and my wonderful clothes meant nothing.

"My gowns!" I reached out for the red silk.

And then he slapped me, knocking me against the wooden headboard so that I saw fragments of light like splintered glass.

"Shut up!"

"But, Frank. . . ." No other words came.

"I told you, shut up!" He hit me again, and I curled up under the bed clothes, tears running into my mouth.

"Don't!" I gasped. "Don't! Please!"

"Then stop whining." He looked at me as if I was nothing. "I need the money. And Christ knows you're no help."

"How *can* I help?" I whispered, frightened, wanting back

what I'd had only days before.

"By keeping out of my way." He piled the gowns over his arm.

"My clothes. What'll I wear?"

"I don't give a damn what you wear. How does that please you? I bought these, and now I'm selling them. Got that?"

I shook my head slowly because of the pain. "I don't understand," I said, fighting for a grip on something that made sense, that I could hold in my hands and know to be real.

"Little spoiled bitch," he said, and then was gone, slamming the door behind him.

What had I done? I wrapped my arms around myself and wept until, worn out, lulled by pain and the heavy fragrance that stole up from the courtyard, I fell asleep.

By morning Frank hadn't returned, and I crept down the stairs to the kitchen, feeling guilty, as if I were to blame for the purple bruises on my face, as if I deserved the marks of Cain.

Otilia, the mulatto woman who cooked and cleaned for Lily, took one look and held out her arms.

"Lord, baby," she exclaimed. "Who done such a thing?"

She was a comfort, a large, soft bosom like I'd never known, and I laid my head on her breast and said nothing.

"There," she said, stroking my hair. "There. Men's a trial. We all know it. And we can't do without them, try as we might."

She pushed me away and looked at the damage. "Coffee," she said softly. "Then you sit here while I see what I kin do."

I sipped the strong, sugary brew she gave me, too exhausted to do anything else. In a short while she was back, humming under her breath.

"You take this," she said, handing me a small, red, silk bag tied with faded gold ribbon. "Maybe it'll work for you."

I examined the little pouch that weighed nearly nothing. "What is it?"

"*Gris-gris*. Made for you. Don't tell nobody, and not that man of yours."

A voodoo charm! I'd been in New Orleans long enough to know about such things — the secret rituals, the orgies, the power of belief in magic when all else seemed hopeless.

I put the little bag in my pocket, ready to believe anything.

"The lousy bastard!"

Lily was sitting beside the bed, holding a cloth to my face.

"He didn't mean it." Why I was defending Frank, I didn't know. It was more like I was shielding myself.

"The hell," Lily said.

"I made him mad. It was my fault."

"He was born mad. And worthless as tits on a boar."

I cringed away from her language and her assessment of Frank's character, but she wanted none of it.

"Get rid of him," she croaked. "Before it's too late."

Of course, I didn't listen. How admit I'd made a mistake? How crawl home, all my foolishness visible in the scars on my face?

She knew I wasn't listening and shook her head sadly. "Here," she said. "Have a spoon of this. It'll make you sleep. And you can keep the bottle. You'll need plenty with that son-of-a-bitch."

It was my first experience with laudanum, but it wasn't my last by a long shot.

"I didn't mean it! Oh, God, darlin', believe me. I wouldn't hurt you. Something got into me, but it wasn't you. Forgive me? Please?"

I was in his arms again, where I belonged, and his lips were kissing away the bruises, wiping out the pain.

"*Shhh,*" I murmured. "It's over. Done. It's all right. I love you."

But it wasn't over. Looking back on my life, I don't know how I survived.

44

Chapter Nine

We left New Orleans in a far different manner than we arrived. Frank had a job tending bar on one of the boats, and, to pay my fare, I was hired on as a chambermaid. The irony didn't escape me as I changed dirty linen and washed out waterclosets and slop jars in those lovely cabins where I'd once been a passenger. I wasn't bitter. I was too tired for that, and too frightened that I'd do or say something to set Frank off. As it was, he'd been unhappy about me having to work for my passage, especially when he discovered that Julian Plummer was aboard.

"Don't get any ideas about servicing the passengers," he warned me as we left. And to make sure that was impossible, he punched me in the eye.

It took two weeks for the swelling to disappear, and by that time we were being put ashore at an unnamed landing somewhere in Arkansas because Frank had been accused — and been found guilty — of marking a deck of cards for a friend, one of the professionals who made a living on the river. It wasn't unusual for the bartender to mark cards, but getting caught was.

"Just my luck," he snarled, as we stood on the muddy bank and watched the boat move away upstream. "Maybe it's you," he said. "The millstone around my neck."

I didn't answer. I was afraid to for fear he'd leave me there without money and with nowhere to go. Mute, I fought down tears as he picked up his bag.

"Come on," he said. "There's got to be a town some place

in this wasteland," and he walked away, leaving me to follow, struggling with my own bag that banged at my legs with every step.

For four years we worked the river towns, moving from one to the next, sometimes by boat, sometimes by wagon, and once even on foot. Natchez, Vicksburg, Memphis, Cairo, sometimes flush, sometimes penniless, me following where Frank led like the beaten dog that I was — without hope, without a thought except the next meal, the next place where I could lie down and lick my wounds.

We were in Natchez when the letter from my mother reached me, informing me of my father's death. The letter was a month old, so there was no question of my going back for the funeral or to take care of Mama in her grief. Besides, we were broke and had been for over a year.

Natchez-Under-the-Hill was crawling with better gamblers than Frank could ever hope to be. He usually fleeced the innocent, the newcomers, and left them wondering what had happened. But in Natchez he was outclassed, and losing made him mean. That day I had a black eye and had stayed in bed in spite of the sultry heat, too miserable to make an effort to wash or to try to disguise my bruises.

I read the letter several times, then crumpled it in a ball, and threw it across the room. My mother was a widow. I wished I was. I wished I was home in that house near the lake where the wind always blew cool, and where innocence was a blessing. Instead, I was sitting here in a filthy boarding house, exhausted, sick from the heat, aching in every bone, and scared that when Frank came in he'd beat me again just to vent his frustration.

I got up and dragged myself to the window, hoping to catch a bit of breeze. None came, but I stayed, leaning on the sill and watching the dock hands load pigs onto a decrepit little river boat, a sad reflection of the floating palaces that traveled the Mississippi. The door slammed, and I held onto the sill, frightened, cowering, beyond helping myself.

"Pack up. We're leaving." Frank's eyes were bloodshot, and his hair hung past his collar.

How many times had I heard those words? When was it that I'd stopped caring? "Where?"

"Saint Louis. I got a job on *Little Bertha* out there. It'll pay your way."

I said: "My father's dead."

He was fishing under the bed for his boots. "Sorry," he said. "But don't expect you can go to the funeral."

"It was a month ago."

He turned around and sat on the floor, looking at me — still in my nightgown, my hair unkempt, my cheeks swollen. "A good thing they can't see you now," he said with a sneer.

"Yes. It is." I bent over the drawer that held what clothes I had left, trying to hide my tears.

"Things'll change when we get some place decent," he said, realizing, too late as always, that he'd been cruel.

I didn't answer. Words had a way of coming out wrong, getting twisted, and used against me.

It was mid-afternoon when *Little Bertha* pushed off against the current, her cargo squealing in the hold. And I knew I'd carry the sound and the stink of those pigs with me the rest of my life — that and the knowledge that the man I'd once loved was now the man I hated with all my soul.

In St. Louis, all the talk was of the Chicago Exposition, and it caught Frank's imagination. "We'll go there," he said. "There's money to be made in a place like that. All those fools come to spend their cash."

I agreed without enthusiasm. One place was as good as another. Except that in Chicago my life changed forever.

★ ★ ★ ★ ★

"Hey, kid. What's the matter?" Joe's voice roused me from what had become a nightmare.

"Nothing." My nose was bleeding again, probably because I'd been crying in my sleep.

"You hurtin'?" He lifted the lantern and peered across at me.

I hurt, all right. The trouble was, I didn't know what hurt worse — my heart and pride, or my body.

"Leave me alone. I'll be fine," I said, fumbling for the bottle in my pocket.

He sat back. "No need to get smart. I was just asking, is all."

His concern hurt me, too. I wasn't used to kindness, didn't know how to respond to it. Only one other person had ever showed me kindness, and that was Dan Sandeman.

Yes, and look where that got you, a voice inside me said. *If it hadn't been for him, you wouldn't be here.*

That was partly true, but I'd learned a valuable lesson from Dan, and maybe more than one. I'd learned I could sing and make money doing it. I'd also learned that Frank's behavior was unacceptable to decent people, to men like Dan.

Well, with any luck, maybe I'd find Dan again. He'd said he was heading West. I wiped my nose on my sleeve. The bleeding seemed to have stopped. Then I looked across at Joe, who was watching me.

"Hey," I said. "I'm sorry. I didn't mean to sound nasty or anything."

"That's okay, kid." He leaned his head against the side of the car. "I'm putting out the light. That all right with you?"

I nodded. Perhaps in the dark sleep would come more easily.

48

Chapter Ten

I was walking down one of the small side streets of the Chicago World's Fair grounds, and I was singing. Alone, I was often happy and able to forget my circumstances. Alone, I could dream, and no one to stop me. Frank had a day job as a shill outside the hall where Little Egypt did her famous hootchy-kootchy dance — it was supposed to be daring, but I thought it was rather silly — and I was free to do as I liked.

I saw every show and exhibit, some over and over. I'd gone back many times to Buffalo Bill's Wild West Show just to watch Annie Oakley, "Little Miss Sure Shot," shoot dimes and playing cards out of her husband's hands, and I always walked through the Women's Pavilion just for inspiration.

There were so many women doing things, making their mark. I saw the actress, Helen Modjeska, and heard a lecture on the rôles of women by Julia Ward Howe. It all made me think, something I usually tried not to do, because then I had to ask myself why I stayed with Frank, why I put up with the beatings, and his reminders of my lack of worth. What I should have questioned was his possessiveness. Why did he want me if I was, as he said, dull, incapable, a millstone around his neck?

It was early June. The sun was warm, and a cool wind was blowing off the lake, and I was simply happy, singing an old French song my grandmother had taught me years before.

"Sur le pont, D'Avignon . . . ," I listened to myself, warbling like a small bird in the midst of the jostling crowd. And then came the words that changed my life.

"Hey! You, Frenchy!"

At first I paid no attention, not making the connection between me and the language of the song. Then a man with a dark, close-trimmed beard stepped in front of me.

"You speak English?"

His question was so unexpected that I laughed.

"Of course," I said. "Why?"

"Where'd you learn to sing? I need a singer bad."

I couldn't remember a time when I hadn't sung. Music was a part of me that I'd denied for the past years. Around Frank I hardly spoke, let alone sang.

I shrugged, avoiding past reminiscences. "I don't know. In school, I guess. And at home."

Brown eyes examined me from head to foot. "Rosalie ran off with a Turk last night. Without her, I'm finished. I'll have to close. You looking for work?"

Although I hadn't admitted it, even to myself, I was feeling useless. Bored. Frank was gone all day, and he gambled at night. I was lonely and restless, especially faced with the example of so many women who were doing worthwhile things.

"Who's Rosalie?" I asked.

He made a face. "My main attraction. And she took off with some guy with a ring in his ear after the last show." He took my arm. Strangely, I wasn't afraid. "Come on in here, and let's see what you can do."

He led me into a false-fronted building. The sign over the door said **Sandeman's Wild West Dance Hall** in red and gold letters. Inside were tables and chairs and a small stage with a painted backdrop of mountains and a sunset sky.

"My show," he said. "It's not Buffalo Bill's, but it won't even be here if I don't replace Rosalie." He handed me a piece of music. "Try this."

The song was "After the Ball." It had premiered at the fair

50

and was on everyone's lips. I knew it by heart, and I put my heart and what I'd learned in my sojourn in New Orleans into that audition.

"Jesus!" he said when I'd finished. "Jesus!"

"What does that mean?" I asked.

"Be here at seven," he said. "First show's at eight. You get ten bucks a night, and you keep the tips. There's always a bunch of guys throwing money."

Ten dollars a night! It was a fortune! I thought of all the things I needed — new shoes, because I'd walked holes in all of mine, silk stockings, maybe even velvet ribbons for my hair.

"What's your name?" he wanted to know. "I've gotta change that sign."

"Pearl," I told him. "Pearl Hart."

He grinned suddenly. "Great name. It'll drag 'em in. All you got to do is get up on that stage and sing. Maybe dance a little. I'll run you through before the show. Hell, Rosalie learned, and if she could, you can. My name's Dan Sandeman. See you at seven, and don't . . . for Christ's sake . . . be late."

I almost wasn't there at all. Frank was enraged when I told him. He paced the floor, and his boot heels sounded like pistol shots.

"You're my wife! I make enough to live on without you going out exposing yourself to every Tom, Dick, and Harry in Chicago!"

He turned and looked at me. Those green eyes I had once thought so beautiful were narrowed into slits.

"Or is that what you want? To be a little whore? God knows, you wouldn't even be good at that, if you act like you've been acting with me."

It was true. The passion of our early days had been left somewhere on the long trail up the river. Along with my pride and my faith in myself, it had been beaten out of me.

"You're wrong, Frank," I protested. "It's not that . . . !"

He cut me off. "You go back and tell this . . . what's his name . . . to forget it. Or I'll do it for you. You're my wife, not some hussy prancing around like those Egyptians."

"It's only till he finds somebody else. Rosalie ran off with a Turk."

The explanation struck me as ridiculous, and I giggled, more from nerves than anything. But it was the wrong thing to do.

He grabbed me and shook me until I thought my neck would snap. "Don't you laugh at me! Don't you ever laugh at me! Understand?"

He'd black my eyes if I didn't answer. I wouldn't be able to go out for weeks. His fingers bit into my flesh. He was strong. And dangerous.

"Yes!" I screamed, not caring who heard. "Yes! . . . yes! . . . yes!"

He let me go so suddenly that I tripped and fell. Lying there at his feet, I was more defenseless than ever, and I covered my face with my hands.

"Shut up!" He kicked at me with the toe of his boot. "Just shut up. You'll have the whole damn' street in here."

Anger, pain infected me. "Whose fault is that?" With the prize of independence uppermost in my mind, I shouted at him for the first time, and it roused his fury even more.

"Yours! You come in and tell me you have some kind of job, cavorting on a stage. You *tell* me. You don't even ask my permission. Who in hell do you think you are?"

I rolled away and struggled to my feet. It was best to put a little distance between us. "I'm your wife," I told him, keeping my voice down, though it shook with anger. "I'm a person, just like you are."

"Person!" he mimicked. "Person. I pay the bills, in case

you hadn't noticed. And I want you here when I come home. Somebody has to keep an eye on you, since you can't seem to do it yourself."

I remembered the jewelry and the dresses we'd sold to pay Frank's debts. I remembered the lice-infested boarding houses in all those river towns. Sure, he paid the bills, but I was the one who went begging. I couldn't speak for the words crowding into my throat — and for the knowledge that, if I did manage to get them out, he'd beat me worse than before.

Instead, I unbuttoned my blouse and looked at the bruises he'd left on my arms — huge, purple welts, spreading over white skin.

"I hope Rosalie's gown has long sleeves," was all I said.

"What in hell are those marks on your arms?"

I was standing in front of Dan, dressed in Rosalie's costume that was too big and made me look like a clown.

"Marks?" I stalled for time to think.

"Oh, Christ! Who's been at you? Your boyfriend? Your pimp? Don't lie to me. I've got enough problems." He ran his fingers through his hair and glared at me.

"Nobody. This dress is too big."

"Can you fix it?"

"I'll try."

I thought I'd distracted him, but, as I discovered later, he was rarely, if ever, distracted. He came close and put his hands on my shoulders. They were big hands, warm, oddly gentle. "Listen to me," he said. "No decent man hits a woman. Got it?"

I nodded. "It's all right," I said. "Really, it is."

"Crap!" He examined my bruises. "Are you nuts, letting some guy do this to you?"

Loyalty won out. Loyalty and some idea that I had to keep

from looking like a fool. "He's my husband," I said. "And I'm not a whore."

"Oy. A husband who beats his wife. And I had to hire her." He put his hands on my shoulders again. "You tell this husband . . . he puts marks on you again, he'll have to answer to me. Dan Sandeman. And maybe to the police. You hear me?"

"I hear you," I said, knowing that I would never repeat his words to Frank. He'd be so angry he'd really hurt me, and then what? I couldn't go home again. Nobody there would believe me, or if they did, they'd say it was my fault. That I'd driven Frank to violence. That I'd made my choice and had to stick to it. Everything was always the fault of the woman. Or so all the women — and men — that I knew always said.

"Where's a needle and thread?" I asked Dan. "We haven't got all night."

I sang for Dan Sandeman that summer and into the fall, sometimes accompanying myself on the guitar. I sang the ballads of Stephen Foster, "Daisy Belle," and "After the Ball." I sang the songs I'd heard and memorized in New Orleans, and I danced, picking up my skirts to show the red shoes and black lace stockings that had been my first purchases.

"What's that husband of yours say about those stockings?" Dan wanted to know.

"I didn't tell him." And I wasn't about to. The memory of my lovely red dress burned deep.

"Pretty little thing like you," Dan said. "Why don't you leave him?"

I shook my head. How could I explain my own worthlessness to this man who believed I was someone else, someone capable? I'd end up sounding as foolish as I was.

"He needs me," I said, sounding foolish even to myself.

It was Dan's turn to shake his head. "Oh, baby," he said, "you don't know anything about need."

He cupped my chin in one big hand and stared at me, and for a minute, it seemed, I couldn't breathe, couldn't think or move away. It was like he had hypnotized me, caught me in a spell.

Finally I said: "Don't . . . ," in a voice that sounded like it came out of a ghost. Maybe it had. Maybe it came out of that other Pearl, the one he thought was there.

He dropped his hand. "I hope I'm around when you grow up," he said, and left me standing alone.

I turned my salary over to Frank who had no way of knowing about the tips I got for singing encores and requests. That money I hid deep in the toe of an old boot, because, although I hadn't admitted it to myself at first, the possession of money gave me power. With enough money, one day I might go free.

But with the closing of the fair, I was out of a job. Dan had packed up and gone, not without asking me to accompany him.

"We'd make a good team," he said. "How about it?"

I shook my head. Freedom, as yet, was a frightening thing. "Maybe some day," I said, blinking back tears. I had grown fond of Dan in spite of his brusqueness, his constant cussing. Sometimes I wondered if I loved him, but I couldn't be sure. I'd thought I loved Frank once, and look where that had gotten me.

"I'm headed to Arizona," he said. "You need me, I'll be out there somewhere."

I threw my arms around him. "I'll miss you."

"I'll miss you, too, kid, and that's a fact." He kissed me then, a hard, lingering kiss, and I responded in spite of myself. There was a tenderness in him that lured me, soothed me, gave me a confidence that had been wiped away by experience.

He pushed me away. "You're a damned dangerous woman," he said. "You know that?"

"Don't make fun," I told him, still fighting tears.

He sighed. "You're also a damned idiot. But like I said . . . I'll be out there, if you need me."

"Maybe some day," I said. "Maybe."

"I'm not holding my breath." He picked up his bag and walked off down a street that, only a few weeks before, had been filled with people and music, laughter and fun. It took all my strength not to run after him, not to call out his name.

It was his farewell kiss that precipitated my flight.

Frank had spent the afternoon drinking and was dressing for a night's gaming. As usual, I was helping him, laying out his shirt, brushing his good black coat, hoping he'd notice and praise me for once.

Instead, he looked at me in the mirror. "Where'll we go now that the fair's over?" he asked.

I shook my head. "I don't know." Without thinking I said: "Dan went out West. Arizona." It was the wrong thing to say.

"Dan!" he snarled. "He's all you can think about. You act like *he's* your husband."

"I didn't mean. . . ." I walked around to the other side of the bed.

"Just what did you mean?"

"Well . . . there's all those boom towns out there. Lots of money in them. We could take a train and be in Denver or even San Francisco in a few days."

"And you could catch up to your boyfriend."

"He's not!" I insisted. "Really." But then I remembered that farewell kiss, and it must have showed on my face.

"You little whore," Frank said.

"I'm not. Please. He was my friend. That's all." I backed away from him, but bumped into the dresser.

"Don't tell me your lies. You let him, didn't you? You spread your legs for the-son-of-a-bitch!"

56

"Please, honey!" I heard myself whimpering, and hated myself for it. "Please. I didn't do anything."

I tried to climb across the bed, but he grabbed my ankles and hauled me off. I tried to shield my face with my hands, but he pulled them away and slapped me hard, on one cheek and then the other, and the diamond ring he wore ripped open my nose.

It was my blood, dripping onto my blouse, spattering the floor. My blood. My life. I screamed.

He didn't hear. He was hypnotized by his own brutality. He punched, kicked, slapped me, until I fell on the floor and curled myself into a ball.

Maybe it was my blood, or maybe it was the sounds I was making, like a frightened rabbit. I'm not sure why — maybe I never will be sure — but he came at me then, not even stopping to take off his trousers, came at me, battered his way into me, and raped me.

"Maybe now you'll remember who you are," he said. He rolled off me and lay still.

Who was I? I was hate. I was a pile of bloody rags, an aching in the place where my heart had been. With what strength I could summon, I kicked him in the groin, not once, but twice.

"You son-of-a-bitch," I whispered. "You son-of-a-bitch," and was happy when he groaned, vomited, and passed out.

I should have killed him then and saved myself further trouble — stabbed him with a knife, throttled him until his eyes bugged out. Instead, I crawled to my feet and left him, face down in his own filth. Then I packed up and ran for my own life.

Chapter Eleven

That night lasted forever. Between the pain and the memories, I slept little. And in the morning Joe found out I was a woman. There wasn't any way to hide the fact, and I nearly died of shame.

"God damn," he said. "I thought you were too puny for a boy. What about the rest? Were you lying or telling the truth? Not that it matters."

"The truth."

"Beating up a girl," he grumbled. "You did right, leavin'." He pulled a piece of jerky out of his pocket and offered it. "You got gumption. I admire that in a woman."

I refused the jerky, hoping he didn't start admiring too much.

Surprisingly, he chuckled. "Don't worry, kid. I like my women all in one piece and in fancy skirts. You ain't exactly a pretty picture right now."

I was sure of that. My head ached, and my face felt swollen, but there was nothing wrong with my mind. I fished out another can of tomatoes. Then I attempted a smile. "My name's Pearl," I said. "Can I go with you as far as Arizona? I promise I won't be any trouble."

He gave me a look that said he knew exactly what I was doing. "Just like a female," he said, taking the can. "But all right. I never walked off and left a lady in distress, and I'm not doin' it now. But take my advice and stick to being Pete till you get where it don't matter."

We arrived in Phoenix a week later. I was still dressed in

58

Frank's clothes with a belt wrapped twice around my waist to hold up my trousers. I stumbled across the tracks at the depot, squinting in the sudden sunlight.

The valley around us was rimmed by mountains, great, rock fists thrusting into the sky, and everything seemed to shimmer in the late afternoon light. The air was soft, fragrant with the scent of flowers I couldn't name, and I stood there in the warmth, in the space that seemed to go on forever, and felt I was shedding a skin, becoming a new Pearl, a woman without a past, ready to begin again. I felt it — the seed of happiness, of possibility, and I laughed out loud for the first time in what must have been years. I was home. I belonged in this place of sand, mountains, cloud shadows. I laughed, standing there in the dusty street in Frank's clothes, with sore ribs and a dirty face, my hair matted on my head like an old carpet.

Joe stared at me as if he thought I'd lost my mind. "Now what?" he asked.

"Now . . . something to eat, a bath, clean clothes, a soft bed," I said.

He shook his head. "We'll have to pinch some food somewhere. Then we'll worry about the rest of it. Maybe find a barn to bed down in till we get our bearings."

I dug into my sack. "We aren't pinching anything, and I'll be damned if I'll spend another night in a straw pile. We can pay our way."

"You mean you have money?" His eyes, bright blue, were wide.

"Enough for a meal and a couple of rooms if we don't get greedy."

"You should've told me."

"We didn't have any place to spend it. Now we do. Let's go." I handed him ten dollars.

"What's this for?"

"Call it thanks. You saved my life."

"Hell," he said. "You were good company."

"So were you," I told him. "The best."

He shuffled his feet in their worn out brogans, and didn't look at me. Then he said: "Maybe we should stick together. We make a pretty good team."

Dan Sandeman had said the same thing, and I'd let him go on without me. Funny, I thought, how two such different men had been my friends, my partners. And how different they both were from Frank! With them I was like the person I wanted to be. How had Joe put it — a woman with gumption? That being the case, I needed to survive on my own. If I had a second chance at life, I needed to prove that I could live it without help. Once more I shook my head and smiled.

"I have to do it by myself," I said to him. "Thanks, anyhow."

"Hell, it was just an idea." He glanced around. The sun was dropping behind the mountains, and the air had turned cool. "Best get settled some place. This country can get cold at night this time of year."

We were walking through what I learned was the Mexican section of town. The houses were adobe with blue-painted doors and windows, and the yards were filled with trees and flowers. Children played there, and chickens scratched in the dirt. The scent of food cooking hung in the air.

My mouth watered. I hadn't had a decent meal since leaving Chicago. At the thought I walked faster. "Come on," I urged. "Let's find a hotel."

"You figure they'll let you in, lookin' like that?" he asked.

I glanced down at my blood-stained shirt, the trousers covered with straw, dirt, everything I'd sat and slept in for a week, and I wanted to cry. Of course, no decent place would have me! Then I caught myself. A fine way to begin living —

sobbing in the street. I had money, and there had to be a store in town.

"Come on," I said. "We're going to find us a horse trough to wash in and some new clothes."

Chapter Twelve

From the little farming community of Pumpkinville, Phoenix had risen, like the bird for which it was renamed, to become the territorial capital. Around the town were fields of squash, lettuce, and beans that were watered by irrigation canals. There were orchards, orange and lemon trees with fruit hanging like lanterns among the leaves, and trees whose names I didn't know, but whose branches made thin, green magic against the sky. The town itself had hotels, stores, churches, doctors, grocers, and lawyers who helped the farmers fight over water rights to the Salt and Verde Rivers that kept the canals flowing. And, as I discovered, like all frontier towns, it had a busy gambling and saloon district.

The bruises on my face were fading. With enough powder, I was able to disguise them and appear almost like my old self, except that the old Pearl was gone, replaced by a woman determined to make her own way.

Joe took the money I'd given him and disappeared. Two days later he returned much richer.

"Grubstake," he explained. "What those guys don't know about poker. . . ." He laughed. "I'll be off soon as I find out when the stage leaves. Sure you don't want to come along?"

"I'm sure. I'll find a job somewhere," I said, sounding more certain than I was.

"Doin' what?"

I'd been thinking about that as I walked the city. "Singing," I said. "I sang at the World's Fair. Why not here?"

He studied me across the breakfast table. Then he said:

"There's women crawlin' all over the saloons in this town. They're dealin', pourin' drinks, some of 'em even try to sing. The gal I heard last night at the Valverde got booed off the stage. If you can carry a tune, I'd say you got a real good chance."

"You can bet on it," I said, annoyed at his doubt.

"My money's on you every time, Pete." He pushed back his chair and stood there, looking awkward. Finally he picked up his hat and put it on. "Good luck," he said. "See you around, maybe."

I was going to miss him. I knew it. Was I doing right, staying in Phoenix alone? Only time would tell. "Go on," I said. "Get out of here before we make fools of ourselves. And thanks for everything."

He did as he was told, and I watched him walk across the room, a cocky man, not handsome, but sure of himself. Little did I think that, within a few years, he and I would be partners in a wild adventure, would once again be on the run, this time with the law on our trail.

Now, truly, I was on my own, and in spite of my determination I was scared. The years spent with Frank had left scars — on my body, and inside where no one could see. He'd told me I was worthless so often that, down deep, I believed it, no matter what I'd done to prove my worth.

You're a dangerous woman. Dan's words came back to me. Well, at least he'd believed in me, given me a chance. I squared my shoulders, figuring I had to save myself. Either that or crawl back home and listen to the I told you so's until I died. But I've never been a quitter. Lots else maybe, but not that. I was on my own and would make the most of it.

That afternoon I went shopping and spent almost the last of my money on an elegant, green walking-costume decorated with black braid, a matching hat with a green ostrich-feather plume, a simpler dress of white *peau de soie,* and a fringed and embroidered Spanish shawl. With luck I'd soon be working again and not have to worry about my rapidly vanishing cash. I crossed my fingers and went back to the hotel to change clothes.

An hour later I pushed open the cut-glass doors of the Valverde Saloon and walked up to the bar. The sudden silence in the room behind me told me the effect my entrance had had. Although my knees were shaking, I managed to sound confident when I spoke to the bartender, a huge man with a mashed-in nose. "I'd like to speak to your boss," I said.

He stared at me like he was trying to make sense out of an unaccustomed situation. Finally he asked: "What for?"

I tilted my chin and did my best to look arrogant. "Personal business."

He chewed on that for a minute. "He ain't here."

"Then I'll wait. Where is his office?"

"You can't wait in there. Nobody goes in there without Mister Burke says."

He was big, loyal, and dumb. Probably had his brains mushed in the ring. I'd seen a lot of men like him and knew he could be gotten around. So I smiled — and lied. "I have an appointment," I said. "And I can't very well wait in here."

Behind me the patrons were hanging on every word. One of them called out: "Do what the lady says, Huey. She can't stand at the bar all day!"

I turned and looked at a bunch of grinning faces and smiled my thanks. To Huey I said: "You see? Now, if you'll be kind enough?"

He gave in, tossing the rag he'd been using to polish the bar onto a shelf.

The office was little more than a storeroom filled with kegs

64

of beer and crates of whiskey. Two chairs and a small desk stood against one wall, and a window faced into the alley. I looked out and saw the cribs across the way, closed at that hour, their occupants sleeping off the excesses of the night before. Inside each was a woman who sold herself for whatever price she could get. I'd seen those women, some of them old, some of them not even able to speak English. Whatever dreams they had were gone now, shattered by alcohol, drugs, the pitiful act that took the place of love.

No matter what, I thought, *no matter what* that will never be me. *Never!* I turned back into the room and sat on one of the rickety chairs, praying my face and my story of half-truths would find me a job.

"You lookin' for me?" The man stood in the door, gawking.

"Mister Burke?"

"Yep."

"I'm Pearl Hart. You've probably heard of me." I held out my hand the way I imagined a queen — or an opera singer — would do.

He took it and held it, wondering what to do next.

"I see you haven't," I said, pulling away and wishing I could wipe my fingers on my skirt. "Well, Phoenix *is* a little out of the way, I guess. But growing. I am a singer. I've been at the Chicago World's Fair since it opened, singing with the Sandeman Company. And I understand that you're in need of an entertainer here."

He stalled for time. "Well. . . ."

I took matters into my own hands. "Mister Burke," I said, "I'll sing for you. You can make up your own mind." Without giving him a chance to reply I stood up and sang that sad and lovely ballad, "After the Ball." It had brought me luck before. Perhaps it would again.

When I'd finished, the applause began. Burke had forgotten

to close the office door, and my admirers from the saloon had crowded near to listen.

"We ain't heard singing like that since we been here," one of them said.

"Give her a job, Burke," said another. "Hattie's got a tin ear. Besides, she ain't much to look at."

I bowed at my audience, then looked at Burke, tilting my head so that the green plume swept past my cheek. "Well, Mister Burke?"

"I think we can make a deal here." He offered me a chair. "Sit down, Miss er . . . ?"

"Miss Hart," I supplied. "Miss Pearl Hart of Chicago."

"Great name."

"So everyone says." I took a deep breath. "My salary for the Sandeman Company was fifty dollars a week," I said. Then added: "Payable in advance, of course."

Burke's eyes bulged. "Well now . . . ," he began, "well, now . . . like you said, this ain't Chicago. I can't afford big city prices."

The old tightwad! I'd done my homework. The Valverde was the classiest saloon in town, and he could afford twice that.

I stood up. I'd learned enough about bluffing from Frank to keep my face expressionless. "What a pity." I offered my hand once more. "If you'll excuse me, I have an appointment down the street."

"Well, now . . . ," he repeated himself, stalling for time. "Don't run off, Miss Hart. Sit down, sit down. I think we can come to an agreement."

I fought down my anger. He thought he was going to get around me because I was a woman who had come to him for a job. The signs were all over him. I decided to take a risk.

"You heard me sing. So did your customers. Fifty dollars

in advance, Mister Burke, or I go to your competitors and take those men with me."

Of course, he agreed. He needed a drawing card, and I was it. And I'd learned a valuable lesson, one I should have been taught earlier. That was, never to sell myself short. Miss Pearl Hart was a quick study.

Chapter Thirteen

It seems that nothing in my early life came without a struggle. I'd been working for three weeks and making good money, when I got up one morning feeling sicker than I'd ever felt. As the day wore on, the symptoms passed, and I was almost well by the time I dressed for work that evening. But the next morning the sickness returned, and the morning after that, and it was with dread that I finally realized I was with child. Frank's child! Conceived on that bitter, brutal night in Chicago. And I was alone with no one to help, on my own with a life growing inside me.

I tried to picture it and failed. Childbirth had never been discussed in my presence. The women I knew usually went into retirement as soon as they began to show, returning to public life only after the baby was born. I'd been too young to remember Maud's birth. In fact, I was sent out of the house for the event, coming home after it was over and Maude lay fussing in her crib.

What did it look like? I wondered. Was it boy or girl, and, worse, would it bear the marks of that violent mating? I shuddered at the memory and at the abyss that lay in front of me. What to do? I supposed I could go home and lay my problems in my mother's lap, but that meant I'd be where Frank could find me, if he was looking. And I'd be a hawk in a cage, stifled, forever trying to spread my wings. I'd be clothed, fed, cared for, but at what cost?

A swift calculation, and I knew I had at least another two months before I had to stop working. If I was lucky, if I saved enough, I'd be able to manage on my own until the child came. I'd find a cheaper place to live. The hotel was a luxury I couldn't afford. And there might be other jobs I could take, at least for a while. I would stay where I was and hope. A glance in the mirror showed me still slender enough to get by. The face that looked back at me seemed hardly old enough to be that of a mother. My skin was unlined. My hair, still short, curled next to my cheeks, giving me the look of a saucy boy. Only my eyes had changed. Gray as slate, they were wary and full of the bitter knowledge that every freedom comes with a price.

That night I finished my last number and sang a few requests. As usual, the Valverde was packed full of men who came to hear me, who elbowed each other away from the stage and fought for the privilege of buying me a drink and maybe walking me home. I accepted the drinks — that was part of the job — except what I drank was the strong, sweet tea Huey kept in a separate bottle under the bar. The other invitations I refused with a smile.

Huey had appointed himself my guardian. It was like having a huge and ugly mastiff who walked beside me and kept strangers away. Every night he left the bar for the length of time it took to see me home. He rarely spoke during the walk except to say as he left: "There. You're all right now."

With him along I never worried. I looked at the stars, more stars than I ever knew existed, and, when the moon was bright, our shadows accompanied us, long and dark on streets turned to silver. In the distance the mountains glimmered. They seemed like animals asleep in the moonlight, and, looking at them, I was happy, free to feel things, to do as I chose, not what someone else decreed.

I was wearing the white *peau de soie* dress with the ruffled neckline, and I had a scarlet geranium tucked between my breasts. I bowed, and smiled, and opened my arms to my audience in an effort to share my pleasure. And then I saw him — in the shadows against the wall where the light from the lamps never quite reached. Those green eyes of his met mine, and there was mockery in them. And desire. And something else I couldn't name.

I think I said, "Frank," and then stood there, open armed, unable to move. How had he found me? I couldn't think, but ran off the stage and into the alley where a few whores still sat in their doorways, smoking, half-dressed, most of them ugly even in the half-light.

"What's yer hurry, honey?" one of them called, and the others cackled like crones, the sound following me like a bad omen.

He caught me before I reached the corner, one hand gripping my arm and spinning me around to face him.

I snarled like an animal. "God damn you! Let me go!"

"Stop!" he commanded. "Stop fighting. I'm not going to hurt you."

"Oh, no. You'd never hurt me, would you, you son-of-a-bitch?" I was back in Chicago, choking on my own blood, struggling for my life.

"It's me, darlin'," he said. "It's me."

I laughed then. It sounded like the laughter of the old whores — used-up and mirthless. "Of course, it's you," I said. No one else had ever called me "darlin'" in that tone that was like a kiss.

"Miss Pearl?" Huey had followed me. Next to his bulk, Frank looked small, unable to hurt anybody.

"It's all right," I said, imagining a street brawl and me in the middle.

"You bet it's all right," Frank intervened. "I'm her husband."

Huey turned to me, his forehead wrinkled. "That true?"

I hated to admit it. "Yes," I said. "Yes, he is."

He shook his head, looking more than ever like a bewildered watchdog. "I'll get back then?" It was a question.

I nodded. "Go on. And thank you." I watched him lumber off and wished I'd asked him to stay.

Frank whistled. "Jeezuz . . . where'd you find him?"

"None of your business. How did you find me?"

He grinned, a cocky gesture that made me want to scream. "Your mother."

Oh, God! My mother! I'd written to her, as I had from the very beginning, saying that she wasn't to worry, that I was in Phoenix and had a good job. In it were lies and half-truths, everything sugar-coated the way I had always done. She knew nothing about how I'd lived. She wouldn't have believed me if I told her.

"What did you do? Play the betrayed husband? Cry on her shoulder? I know your tricks, all of them, so you better tell me."

"I told her we had a fight," he said, sounding humble in the face of my accusations, not at all like the man I'd known. "I told her I loved and missed you. That I wanted you back." His voice broke, but I wasn't about to be taken in so easily.

"I didn't miss you," I said. "I didn't miss a bloody nose or black eyes, either." I turned and started to walk away.

He was beside me. "Please. You don't understand. I love you, darlin'. When I found you were gone, I went crazy. I turned Chicago upside down, trying to find you. To make it up to you."

I set my chin. "I'll bet," I said, but part of me was listening, wondering if what he said was true and thinking of the child that lay, helpless, inside me.

"Can't we try again?" He was pleading now. "You don't

71

know how sorry I am. Please say yes. I won't lay a hand on you. Except . . . ," he smiled, and the moon touched his face, lighting the hunger in his eyes, "except to love you."

I remembered how our bodies had once melted and fused from the lightning strike of passion. I remembered, and it seemed a long time since I had felt the touch of a man's hands, the feel of his lips. I was young. And lonely in spite of the audience of males to whom I sang. I sang about love, but I was empty.

I pulled my shawl tight and looked up at him. "We'll have to talk," I said. "But not here, and not now. I'm tired. I'll meet you for breakfast. Not before ten. I sleep late these days."

His face sagged with relief. "Think about this, Pearl," he said. "I've changed. I'll never hurt you again. You can believe it. Remember the good times. We'll have them again, you and me. We're meant to be."

"Good night, Frank," I said, and left him standing there, his hat in his hands.

I didn't sleep for hours, replaying scenes from our marriage over and over. Could I believe him? Had he really reformed? I tried to count the times he'd sworn the same thing to me, but there were so many times, and me bruised and bleeding but wanting so desperately to believe him. But children needed a father. If I took Frank back, we would be a family, and if, indeed, he had turned over a new leaf, my worries about supporting myself would be over. I got out of bed and went to the window, stood watching the moon as it hovered in the west and then disappeared, leaving an emptiness in the sky.

Finally I climbed back into bed and curled up like a miserable child. "Maybe he *has* changed," I whispered to myself. "Maybe this time he means it."

By morning I'd made up my mind, and, when Frank came

in and sat down at my table, I felt I was in full command of the situation.

"I've been thinking about this all night," I began truthfully. "And there's something you should know. I'm . . . I'm with child, and it's yours." I sat back and watched and waited. His response would determine what happened next.

He was shocked and, for a moment, couldn't speak. "A child," he stammered finally. "A child. Mine."

"Yes. It happened in Chicago. More's the pity."

He put his elbows on the table and buried his head in his hands. "Oh, God. I'll make it up to you. You will let me?" He sounded like a child himself, caught in a situation he couldn't control.

"As I said, I've thought about this. A child needs a father and a family. This one will have to make do with us. Such as we are."

He looked up then, and it almost seemed as if the past hadn't happened, as if he were the young pirate I'd so loved. My heart skipped a beat. *Maybe*, I thought. *Maybe.*

"Believe me, darlin'. I'll do my best. I'll take care of you both, and that's a promise."

I'm sure he believed what he said, that his intentions were honest. He was a man who could convince himself, and others, of anything. That morning he convinced me, who should have known better. But, like him, I wanted to believe, and in the wanting forgot all the hard-won lessons of our past.

It was so good to be in his arms again, to feel him against me like a pulse. That afternoon we wiped out all the horror of memory and began again in the present, in delight that lifted me, carried me until I fell back, exhausted, onto the pillow.

Too soon it was evening. I pushed myself out of bed and went to the washstand and heard Frank stirring.

73

"What're you doing?" he demanded, sitting up suddenly.

"Getting ready for work." I sighed. I'd much rather have gone back to bed.

"Work!"

I cringed at the sound of that one word and took hold of the dresser for support. It wasn't . . . *couldn't* be starting again so soon. "I have a job," I said timidly, and cursing myself for it.

"I don't want you working. Especially not in that place."

It *would* start. I knew it down in the darkness of my body so recently awakened by desire. It would start and go on and on, a whirlpool that sucked me down and spit out the pieces. But only if I let it. I took a firm grip on the carved wood and faced him.

"I'll quit when you get a job, and not before," I said.

His head snapped up like I'd hit him. "What in hell does that mean?"

I took a deep breath. "It means just what I said. It means I can't live like before, always on the edge, always worried about money and having to sell my clothes just to eat. It means I can't stand never knowing when something awful is going to happen, when you'll hit me because your luck's gone bad. It means I want a home for us and our child like you promised. I want some kind of security. You said you've changed. Now I want proof. And I'll keep on working until I can't any more. That's all." I felt my legs start to tremble. I had never talked back to him in my life.

He looked at me for a long time, not saying anything. Then, abruptly, he got up.

"All right," he said. "We'll try it your way. But I'm coming along tonight, and every night, just to keep an eye on you. And you can tell that goon who was with you he isn't needed any more."

"Huey's a good guy," I said, turning to pour water into the basin. "He can't help how he looks."

Frank clipped the end off a cigar, lit it, and came to stand beside me. "That's not the point," he said. "The point is, you have me now."

Why, I asked myself as I dressed, didn't that fact make me feel happy?

Chapter Fourteen

Frank's promises lasted exactly six months. He was unable to find a job that suited him, or to keep any job longer than a few weeks. We lived off what I earned at the Valverde. But when the child began to show, beyond what was considered decent, I had to quit and stay home in the little house we'd rented, and watch my carefully hoarded savings dwindle.

Everything that had frightened me was happening again, only this time it was worse. This time there was a child to consider, another life, and for the moment I was helpless to do anything except urge Frank to find — and keep — a job.

"God damn it!" He was shouting the way he always did when I made him aware of his imperfections. "You're turning into a nag. Just shut up, can't you?"

"I won't!" I was clearing up after breakfast and was already exhausted. Inside me, the child seemed heavy, a constant weight that made my back and shoulders ache and shortened my temper. "I won't shut up. And I don't intend to end up on the street, either. Maybe I'll just go home."

There was always the possibility of going back to Toledo, and it scared him — the notion that I might talk, and others would learn just what kind of black sheep he really was.

"That's it! Run back to your mother," he sneered. "Tell her I'm a failure. Then tell her how you've been singing in a saloon. She'll be happy to hear about that."

"Better sing than starve!" I slammed the dishes down. "Is that what you want? To see your wife and child go hungry while you play silly card games with a bunch of losers and crooks?"

76

I shouldn't have said it. As soon as the words came out of my mouth, I knew I'd gone too far.

He slapped my face with all his strength. I felt the blow travel down my backbone, and I wrapped my arms around my belly where the baby lay, heavy as a stone.

"The baby!" I screamed at him. "Please! The baby!"

He put his hands around my throat, and I saw his face. It was distorted, the face of a madman.

"That's all you think about!" he yelled. "The baby. What about me?"

He was jealous! The truth dawned, even as I fought for breath. He was jealous of an unborn child, of anyone who seemed to take his place. What would he be like with the reality of it — the crying, the instinctive demands of a new life?

I closed my eyes so as not to see him. "You're the father," I croaked around the pressure of his fingers. "It's yours, too."

"Christ!" He dropped his hands and shoved me against the wall. "You don't have to keep reminding me."

I kept quiet, even while he went to the crock where I kept our money and took out a fistful of bills.

Let him go, I thought. Just let him go. And was relieved when he went out without a look or a word, banging the door behind him.

The pain struck an hour later. I was in the tiny yard, trying to calm myself, trying to think, but my mind kept floating off in all directions, making and discarding plans, fighting with itself over words both spoken and left unsaid. And then the pain came, a huge, internal motion, like a fist of fire, a boulder demanding release from the bowels of earth. It was too soon! The child would be born only to die. And then I laughed hysterically, fighting the agony and the hope. If it died, I would be free again to run away and hide. That's what I thought, and I am still ashamed for wishing death on my sweet first-born.

Angelita, my neighbor, found me clinging to the fence between our yards. Quickly she got me inside and to bed and then did whatever was necessary while I lay, half conscious, riding the crest of the pains, hating them, wanting to be free of the burden that was hammering within.

Little Joe was born the next morning. He was big for an eight-month child, and lusty, demanding food and attention at the top of his lungs. I took one look at his red face, his tiny head covered with damp, black curls, and fell in love. He was mine, this fully-formed person who had struggled to be born, to live, almost against my wishes. He was mine. And I would keep him safe.

Frank didn't come home until late that afternoon.

"Come, meet your son," I called.

He came, looking stunned. "My God. My God," was all he could say.

"He's fine, no thanks to you," I said.

Frank buried his face in his hands. I found his tears repulsive. He was crying, not for what he had done, but for himself.

"Goldwater's Dry Goods is looking for a clerk," I said. "Best go apply for the job."

He looked up then, his face twisted. "Me, selling shoes to old ladies with bunions. Don't you ever stop?"

"No," I said. "I never do. You'll have to live with it."

I pulled Little Joe closer to me, closed my eyes, and fell asleep.

Passion dies quickly without love to sustain it. After Little Joe's birth, all my passion turned to him. I was a tigress mother, fierce and protective, because I worried, always, that Frank's jealousy would turn to abuse, not of me, but of a helpless child. Had that happened, I would have killed him. Unfortunately it did not. He took his vengeance out on me, using force to bed

78

me, taking advantage of the fact that Little Joe's birth had made me weak.

Our daughter, Emma, was born eleven months later. She, too, was the child of a rape, but so delicate, so lovely, that my heart turned over at the sight of her. Whatever happened, I hoped she would never know what I knew of life, of the cruelties that exist between a man and a woman, a husband and wife.

So I made plans. I was going to run away, to Alaska, perhaps, or Mexico, or Ontario where I was born, some place where Frank would never find us. I was still young enough to believe I could cast off selves and live as I chose. Such arrogance I had! Well, I'm glad of it. Without that arrogance and that flame for living, I might not have survived the next five years.

As it turned out, I needn't have worried about a place to hide. In February, 1898, the Spanish blew up the American battleship, *Maine*, in Havana Harbor, and the entire male population of Phoenix, Frank included, talked of nothing but war.

Ready to fight, the men marched, drilled, shouted, and, when war was declared, they went off with Roosevelt's Rough Riders or whatever hastily formed regiment would have them.

Barely concealing my relief at his departure, I waved good bye at the station one hot day in April, and then went home to the children. If God was just, Frank would never return. Most women were praying for the safety of their husbands or lovers. I prayed that a bullet would take him, and I'd be free once and for all.

Chapter Fifteen

A month later I took Little Joe and Emma to my mother in Toledo. My money was almost gone, and there was no way I could go back to work at the Valverde and leave them at home alone most of the night. I had tried working, briefly, as a clerk, taking the children to Angelita when I left. But her five ran wild in the streets and set an example far different from what I wanted for my own.

On the train, going East, the children and I stared out the window, all of us seeing the country for the first time. My first trip had been passed in the dark, and I was amazed at the glittering desert, the empty plains, the prairie that, even then, was still a surging sea of grass, with here and there a town built in response to the arrival of the railroad. And after the towns, more grass, on and on, until it seemed the entire world was a plain that rippled in the wind and seemed to breathe in and out like a tawny animal.

"Big," said Little Joe. "Big. Big. Big." He bounced in his seat a minute, then turned serious. "Papa?" he asked, his eyes wide. "Papa come?"

"Papa's gone to war," I explained as gently as I could.

"What's war?"

"It's men like your papa fighting for their country."

"Fight?" he said. "Like you and Papa?"

His comprehension hurt. Between us, Frank and I had made him a victim. I pulled him onto my lap and kissed his cheek.

"Sometimes grownups get mad," I explained. "But we love you just the same."

He seemed happy with that, and he was happy to meet my mother who was waiting for us at the station. She had tears in her eyes as she welcomed us, but for me it was like meeting a stranger, a woman I hardly remembered, a dream person to whom I had written years of lies. In fact, I hardly recognized myself as I stood there in almost the same spot where I had waited with Frank the night we ran away. Who had I been then? Who was I now? I was twenty-eight years old and had lived through what seemed like a hundred lives, variations of someone named Pearl, a woman whose depths and motivations I still didn't understand.

My initial doubts turned into frustration as I tried to settle back into the surroundings of childhood. The house where I'd been brought up was unchanged: high-ceilinged, cluttered — the way most houses were then — with pictures, figurines, plants, antimacassars, flowered carpets, souvenirs from the many places my father had been in his job with the railroad.

I couldn't breathe in that house where my mother, sister, and their friends gossiped over tea and seances. My mother was ever hopeful that she would make contact with my dead father, Maude praying that she would learn that her future would not be that of unmarried daughter and companion. It wasn't any better outside. The summer was rainy. Dampness rose from the ground and fell from the skies, and I, used to the high, dry atmosphere of the desert, felt stifled, squeezed into myself, as if I were wearing a too-tight corset.

I had had a taste of independence and now discovered that, when you live on another's charity, even that of your family, your independence is given away in exchange for comfort. I would gladly have gone to work to supplement my mother's income. She was living on my father's pension, and having extra mouths to feed stretched her budget. But there were no jobs available, certainly none that suited her visions of propriety.

"I'll manage," she said. "Haven't I always?"

"Of course," I agreed. "But everybody can use extra money."

I was thinking of the tips I'd made just for singing the sentimental songs men loved to hear. I was thinking of the pleasure of being alone with no one to tell me do or don't. I was thinking about the desert and how, when you looked out, you could see a hundred miles to where the sky reached down and curved around mountains like a hand in a blue velvet glove. I was homesick, missing the saguaros that thrust up out of red rock and that, in early summer, wore crowns of white flowers that turned quickly to sweet fruit, the thunderstorms that swept in on a wave of scented air and passed quickly, leaving the arch of a rainbow to be wished upon.

How is it that home means such different things? And how many never find their place of belonging? Through bad judgment and accidents, I had found my home, and it was far from the stifling environment of my childhood. Dimly I knew that if I didn't make an effort, my life was as good as over. I needed silence. The constant, empty chatter of idle women split me into fragments. I wanted, needed to be whole. So, after three weeks, I took a hack to the station and purchased a one-way ticket home.

"But you can't!" My mother was stunned by my plan. "You have children to think of. You can't just go running off. Not again. It isn't done. What will people think?"

Ah, yes. The question of last resort. The question by which I'd been raised. What, indeed? And what, I wondered, would they have thought, those friends, those bastions of virtue, if they had seen me traveling bruised, broken, dressed as a rag-tag boy in a freight car? If they had watched me relieve myself in a dark corner in front of a man? In spite of myself, I grinned at the image of horrified faces, and irritated my mother even more.

"Why can't you settle down?" she wanted to know. "Why can't you be like everybody else? I had such plans for you. But no . . . you never make anything easy. Always hard-headed. Selfish." She stopped for a breath and then went on. "Well, I'll tell you. You aren't taking those babies with you. They stay here with me, and that's the end of it. At least, till you come to your senses. Children need a home. You go on and make a fool out of yourself. You're no lady, I'll tell you that. Running around the country like a gypsy, first with that man you ran off with, and now by yourself."

It was the longest speech she'd ever made, and I knew I was supposed to be chastened. Instead, I was exultant. Little Joe and Emma would be cherished and watched over while I struggled to earn enough money to make them a proper home. It would take time, but I'd learned thrift the hard way. And, besides, fortunes were being made in the West. With any luck at all, I'd have both children with me in no time. Still, my mother's criticism hurt me, and made me angry, too. I wasn't the daughter she'd hoped for, was, instead, a disappointment. But why should I be punished for my differences? I stuck out my chin.

"I can't help what I am," I said. "I can't be like you, but that's not my fault."

She always had the last word. "I hope you don't live to regret it," she said.

It sounded like a curse.

Chapter Sixteen

At the Valverde, all the talk was of the signing of the armistice with Spain. The war, the fighting, was over, and the men would be coming home. I listened to the news with dread, for, although I hadn't heard a word from Frank, I hadn't been notified of his death, either. He'd be back, and the cycle of our marriage would begin again. The thought was more than I could bear. I could, I supposed, file for divorce, but in my bones I was still Catholic enough to fear being a total outcast. There was also my mother, who would never recover from a divorce in the Taylor family. Something had to be done, but what? Circumstances made up my mind for me before the month was out.

There was a new moon. I stood in the alley after work, tilted back my head, closed my eyes, and made a wish the way I used to do as a child. A wish on a new moon was sure to come true, so I mumbled to myself in the dark. "Tell me what to do, and where I'm going."

"Sayin' your prayers, Pearl?" Al Burke had stepped out into the alley behind me.

I was startled. "Where's Huey?"

"Busy. I'll walk a ways with you."

"I'll be all right." Maybe it was only instinct, but I didn't want his company.

"Sure you will," he said. "I'm here to see to it." He was keeping pace with me, though I had begun walking fast. "Guess you were prayin' your man comes home soon."

I answered him with a laugh and kept going. Something in his tone seemed out of place, frightening in the dark alley where usually the whores sat smoking or looking for last-minute customers. That night, however, none of them was out, and the emptiness frightened me even more.

"Slow down," he commanded. "A nice night like this, you ought to enjoy a little walk. Unless . . . unless you got company waiting at home."

"Nobody's waiting," I said. "I'm just tired."

"And wanting a man, I bet. Alone all these months."

I knew then what he was after and turned to run, but he caught me before I'd taken three steps. His hands were rough on my shoulders, and his breath smelled like old cigars and older whiskey. And all I could see in my terror was Frank.

"Get your hands off me!" I yelled, hoping one of the whores would come out.

"Shut up. I'm not going to hurt you." He was breathing hard, his face close to mine. Even in the dark I could see the lust in his eyes, and I struggled to get free, calling for Huey as I did.

But he was a big man and strong. "You been givin' it to Huey?" he panted. "Christ! The Queen of Chicago and Huey!"

The very thought was obscene. I sank my teeth into his wrist and held on like a bulldog. When he tried to shake me off, I raised my knee and let him have it in the groin. And at that moment, Daisy, one of the whores, knocked him cold with what looked like a frying pan. Then she and I stood, looking at each other over the body.

"Is he dead?" I whispered.

She snorted. "It'd take more'n that to kill the son-of-a-bitch." She kicked at him with a bare foot. "He'll have a set of sore balls and a lump on his head in the morning, is all."

"What'll we do with him?"

"I'll take care of it. You'd better skedaddle. And I mean out of town. He'll call the law on you, if I know him."

"But he can't!" I was more than a little stunned and wasn't thinking clearly. "I mean . . . he was . . . he wanted. . . ." I stopped, wordless.

"Yeah," she said. "I know. And he's a big man in town, and you're a gal that sings in a saloon. Better than a whore, but not much. He can say what he wants and make it stick. The law's on his side, honey."

I sat down on the stoop. "Where'll I go?"

She shrugged. "Me, I'm saving to go to 'Frisco. Another year oughta do it."

'Frisco. It sounded like the moon. I put my face in my hands and hoped the whole scene would be blotted out, but, when I looked again, she was still there, and so was Burke's body, looking ugly and bloated in the faint light.

"'Course there's always Silver City," she offered. "And Globe's going to bust wide open with the railroad goin' through. I been thinkin' of that myself." She cocked her head. "Come to think . . . there's a Chinee looking for a cook to go with him up that way. He came around today, asking did any of us want the job."

Globe! It seemed so simple. Everyone had been talking about the railroad and the copper boom. And Joe had gone there with high hopes.

"Globe," I said out loud. And then, curious: "Why didn't you take the job? It's a way out of here." And better than giving herself to creatures like Burke.

She laughed. "Honey, I'd just as soon take my chances with white men. But since you gotta leave, I thought I'd mention it."

The way I saw it, white men weren't any better than any other kind. It was true that the whole country was terrified at the influx of the Chinese. In fact the Chinese Exclusion Act had been passed to keep them out. But under the circumstances

86

I wasn't inclined to worry. I'd hitch a ride to Globe and find Joe. Maybe, by now, he'd struck it rich.

I looked at Burke, lying on the ground, his belly swelling over his belt, and decided I'd take my chances. "Where's the Chinaman now?"

"Said he'd be camped by the river in case anybody changed their mind."

"You won't tell?"

She snorted again. "Nobody's going to tell this bastard a thing. He owns these damn' shacks, but he don't own us."

My mouth dropped open, and she laughed at my surprise.

"Yeah. He collects the rent and anything else he wants. Gets it off for free, the old hog. Don't look so shocked. It could be worse."

"I wish I'd killed him," I said, and meant it.

"You and a bunch of others. Now scram. Like I said, I'll take care of him."

"I don't know how to thank you," I said.

"Shit, honey. We're all in it together. Go on now. I got work to do."

She bent down and took Burke's legs to drag him into the little room she didn't even own, and, as she did, his coat fell open, revealing a wallet stuffed with bills.

"I'll be damned," she said, then darted a look at me.

Although I could have used the money, there exists a certain honor among thieves — and women. "Looks like you'll be going to 'Frisco sooner than you thought," I said with a grin.

"I'll be damned," she repeated, and quick as a snake she reached for the wallet. "You won't turn me in?"

I shook my head. "I'm leaving. And you'd better pack and get to the station before he wakes up."

"You're a real lady." She stuffed the money in her bosom. "I won't forget this."

We stood there in the alley, and the moon turned her dyed-yellow hair to silver.

"Good luck," I said.

She laughed, a harsh sound as if she'd forgotten how. "To you, too," she said. "Now go on and git."

I hiked up my skirts, stepped over Burke's fat body, and went in search of the Chinaman.

Chapter Seventeen

The Chinaman was easy to find with his big wagon and team of mules, and the scent of his opium pipe. I followed the sweetness and found Harry Hu sitting beside a dying fire like a genie or a fairy godmother, his slanted eyes full of wisdom. I loved him at first sight.

"I heard you need a cook," I said, standing there in my fine dress and probably looking to him like one of his pipe dreams.

He made a wide gesture. "Come," he said. "Come, missy, and sit."

I did, and we looked at each other across the coals without speaking. I heard the night hawks crying in the fields and saw the sparks rising overhead, and felt that I, too, was in a dream — me and this little man with eyes that saw everything, but passed no judgment.

He was quiet for what seemed like a year. Then he said: "You cook, missy? You no look like cook."

I wondered what he thought I was. Probably a whore, or a runaway wife. "I manage," I said.

"You have family?" he asked after a minute.

"Yes," I said. "But not here. I'm a widow."

"Ah." The sound was sorrowful, spinning out in the dark like a musical note.

"I'll wash dishes. Serve tables. Anything," I said to break the spell. "I'll work hard for you, I promise."

"Why *fan gwai* lady want to work for me?" he asked.

"What's that? *Fan gwai?*"

He smiled, more to himself than at me. "White ghost," he

89

said, and watched me as the meaning came clear.

I smiled, too. I'd been called worse. "I need a job," I told him. "I want my children with me. I want to earn enough to bring them here. Can you understand?"

Of course, he did. He was Chinese, and revered family, kept a faded photograph of the wife he hadn't seen in twenty years in a gilt frame that hung on the wall of the wagon. He was fleeing persecution in California where anyone not a merchant was either being deported or refused permission to enter the country. In a way we were two of a kind. We'd both been beaten, robbed, been the object of fanatical hatred. And we'd both survived to keep fighting.

I knew none of this that evening, but sensed it, the way one animal can sense another's pain. It was probably against the law for a Chinese to employ a white woman, just as it was illegal for them to marry one. He was taking a chance, and a big one. He sat looking into the embers for a long time, weighing his decision.

Finally he said: "I leave tomorrow. Sun up. You come."

"I'll be here," I promised. "My name is Pearl."

Neither then nor at any other time did we talk about wages. Harry simply paid me at the end of each week, and I put the money into a stocking and kept it in the small trunk that was all I took with me. I thought of banking it, but decided to keep it handy. I was still thinking like a fugitive — to my eventual sorrow.

The history of the Chinese in America isn't pretty. I learned a lot of it first hand, listening to Harry's broken English and watching the sorrow cross his face. He'd come to California in the 'Seventies, hoping to find a job, save his money, and send for his bride. But it didn't turn out the way he'd planned. By the time he managed to do more than earn a meager living, working in the lettuce fields, the Exclusion Act had been passed and women, particularly the prostitutes who had been imported, were no longer admitted to the country. The fact that his wife was a decent person and not one of those poor creatures made no difference.

With the help of a cousin, Harry opened an herb store, dispensing medicines to his own race. But even there, in his little corner of Chinatown, he was suspected of acting as a physician, perhaps even selling abortifacients to white women. His shop was burned, and he hid for weeks in the home of his cousin, fearing for his life.

Letters flew between California and Globe, where another cousin was prospering on a small farm. The mines and smelters were producing, the miners needed to eat, the cousin wrote. Together he and Harry could make a good living and perhaps, one day, when the laws were relaxed, they could send for their wives, those women who were waiting, their hope growing smaller with the passing of each month, each decade.

And so, in a camp wagon drawn by two mules so ancient, so set in their ways, it took a miracle to get them moving, Harry left California, traveling at night, avoiding towns, and praying that he wouldn't be stopped, robbed, or murdered on the road.

How well I understood! As we sat on the wagon seat, piecing together our stories, it became clear to me that the world was a vicious place, and that the abused were everywhere — not just women like me, but entire races of people whose only thought was to stay alive. And if it was unorthodox, even illegal, for a white woman to work side by side with a Chinese, too bad! I'd take the chance and worry about the consequences later.

Chapter Eighteen

Like so many mining towns in the West, Globe had a violent history. The Apaches, now confined to the San Carlos Reservation, had more than once gone on the rampage, determined to keep the white prospectors out of their homeland. Many of the men who went into those lonely mountains in the early years never came out, or did so draped across the back of a mule. The Apache Kid, Al Sieber, Hunky-dory Holmes, Geronimo were still talked about as if they were alive, and so were Big Nose Kate, who'd run a boarding house, and the sainted Nellie Cashman who'd started the Buffalo Hotel and bankrolled miners only a few years before my arrival.

Munson's Chunk had, indeed, existed, as well as the mountain of silver ore that brought miners stampeding into the area, but when I got there, Globe had become a copper mining and smelting town. It was linked to the rest of the world by a network of twisting roads and rough mountain passes suitable only for mule trains, stagecoaches, and wagons. Everyone was waiting for the arrival of the railroad, an event that had been delayed for too long.

Nature had also turned its violence on Globe. Floods, fires, destruction were common occurrences, as I had yet to learn. But on the day when Harry and I arrived and were welcomed by his cousin — a work-hardened little man called, for some odd reason, Gilbert — I knew nothing more than that Globe, nestled in the mountains, was lovely and secluded, and that, if Al Burke tried to find me and jail me for assault, he'd never think of looking in a cook shack run by a Chinese named Harry Hu.

My meals were free. I slept on a pile of quilts in the wagon, but once Gilbert and Harry set up business in an abandoned shed on the banks of Pinal Creek, I slept behind the big iron cook stove hauled all the way from California. I slept warm and untroubled and available to cook a meal for any hungry miner who came along.

And they came in shifts, scoffing up food like starving animals, their elbows plunked on the oilcloth-covered tables, their faces covered with dust from the mines. Gilbert had furnished the tables and benches and set them out under a rude *ramada*. He also supplied vegetables and chickens for the stew pot, the bacon, beans, and beef that disappeared into the bearded mouths of customers almost faster than Harry and I could cook.

Within a month my hands were red and cracked from washing dishes, and my legs ached constantly from long hours at the stove and waiting on tables. But I had no complaints. My bank roll was growing even though I sent a part to my mother every month.

I also kept an eye out for Joe. I asked about him, except that I didn't know his last name. I'd spent two weeks in a railroad car with a man whose full name I didn't know. I had to laugh to myself about that, imagining what the dowagers back in Ohio would have to say.

And then one day I heard a familiar voice. "Pete! I'll be damned!"

I turned, and there he was, as disreputable-looking as the first time I'd seen him — scruffy beard, his hands grimy, his fingernails caked with dirt.

"Can't you clean up before you come to dinner?" I asked with a grin to soften my words.

Actually he looked no worse than the others — the smelter crews, the men who went down into the pits and came up sweating, covered with rock dust and the stains of the red earth.

"That's a fine greeting!" He plunked himself down on a bench and took in my own appearance — the stained apron, my hair pulling loose from its bun, my face red from the heat of the stove and the humidity of the afternoon. "You ain't exactly a sight for sore eyes, neither."

I let that pass. "Hungry?"

"Enough to eat the asshole out of a skunk, begging your pardon. And none of that chop suey stuff." He cocked his head. "What're you doin' slinging hash for a Chinee? It's supposed to be the other way around."

"Earning a living and glad of it!" I snapped.

Early on there had been a lot of comment on Harry and me that I'd ignored. Explanations were useless in a society geared to hatred and fear of the Chinese.

"Don't get all fired up," he said. "I was just curious. What happened to the songbird job?"

I handed him a plate of meat and beans. "Things got uncomfortable, and I left."

"In a hurry like last time?"

"Sort of."

"You get yourself in the damnedest predicaments for such a little critter."

That was true. I sighed. "I'll be out of here some day. I'm saving up."

"You got any spare cash?" He swallowed a mouthful and waited for my answer.

"Some. Why?"

"I was fixin' to ask for a loan."

"How much?"

"Fifty bucks. I've got me a prospect that looks real good.

You get so you know when you're close. You can smell it. But I need a few things to keep going."

He sat there hopeful, and I couldn't count the thoughts that went through my mind. What I said finally was: "How long have you been here?"

He blinked. "You know as well as I do."

"And you haven't hit anything?"

Seeing where I was headed, he raised a hand to stop me. "I had some bad luck, is all. But not this time, and that's a promise."

"Promises don't put food on the table," I said. "What'll you put up as collateral?"

"What do you want?"

"A half share in those diggings you're so proud of."

"Robbery!" he said. "That's what it is."

But I'd learned a few things in the years I'd been on my own, and one of them was that I didn't throw money down a hole in the ground. I sat on the bench across from him. "Who grubstaked you back in Phoenix?"

"I knew you'd bring that up."

"It's true, isn't it?"

He slammed his big hand down flat. "And who got you there? The fact is I damn' near dug myself to death back in those hills. But now I'm onto something. In a couple months we could both be rich."

Could I really believe him? From the look of him, he wasn't any better than a derelict, the kind you saw hanging around train stations, bumming quarters, working in saloons for a place to sleep.

"I'll think about it," I said. "Come back tomorrow." And then I felt mean, like I'd kicked a dog that was begging a handout. "Dinner's on me."

He smiled at that. "I appreciate it."

"We go back a ways," I said.

He pushed himself up and away from the table. "You were good company, Pete."

"It's Pearl now."

"Yeah, well, you're still Pete to me. Scrawny and big-eyed."

Why did those words grab at me? Why did I get sentimental, remembering how he'd helped me, jollied me out of pain. I flapped the dishtowel I was holding at him. "Go on. Git!" I said. "See you at breakfast." Then I turned to the man who'd come in and sat down at the next table.

"What'll it be?"

He smiled, showing white teeth in a face tanned by wind and weather. "Some of that chop suey," he said.

I stared. "You like it?"

"Yes." His eyes glinted, pale blue like the chicory that bloomed in the fields of my childhood.

"Why?"

"It's different. Don't you get tired, eating the same things?"

I shrugged, never having thought about what men put in their stomachs. Chop suey was only a general term for a plate of meat, vegetables, rice or noodles. Harry ate something like it at every meal, and I usually did, too, being too tired to care or notice what I was eating.

"I'm just glad to be eating at all," I said.

He studied me for a minute, those blue eyes going from my head to my feet. Then he said. "You're Pearl Hart. I heard you sing."

That stopped me. "Where?" I asked. "Where'd you hear me?"

"The Valverde. It *was* you?"

I nodded slowly, wondering if he was a cop put on my tail by Al Burke.

"Would you sing for me?"

96

I looked him over carefully. He was well dressed, a cut above the usual diner, and obviously used to spending a lot of time outdoors. Probably not a cop, I decided. "It'll cost you," I said, and then was ashamed. He was earnest, and the look in his eyes was honorable. And there I was, greedy as a whore, demanding payment for a few minutes of pleasure. "I'm sorry," I said. "What would you like to hear?"

"I leave that to you." His smile came again, slowly, shivering over his face like a ripple over a pool of still water, and making me tremble inside like he'd peeled off my skin and scratched my bones.

"I'll get your dinner first," I said, and rushed into the cook shack where Harry was chopping vegetables.

"He wants chop suey," I said, my heart still fluttering. "And he wants me to sing."

Harry raised an eyebrow. "So-o-o," he answered, drawing out the syllable and sounding pleased. "Sing pretty, then."

"You don't mind?"

He was astonished. "Mind? Mind? To sing, to make music is gift. Not to sing, very bad thing."

I gave up trying to figure out his logic, took off my apron, and smoothed my hair, and wished I had one of my pretty gowns — all because a stranger with blue eyes and hair the color of wheat had noticed me. I sang "After the Ball," always a favorite, and Pinal Creek splashed and murmured, and the sky in the west turned the color of an old fire, fading away as the last notes faded, leaving us in twilight that seemed heavy with ghosts and old sorrows.

Several men had stopped to listen, and they applauded and whistled. "More!" someone yelled. "Sing some more!"

They were lonely, I realized, and starved for pleasure, and never mind that the saloons on Broad Street kept open night and day and had music aplenty. Many of them had left families to come and slave in the mines or in hope of a strike of their own, earning money to take back to their wives and children. I understood, and so I sang — and sang, until the stars came out and the moon rose over the Natanes Plateau like a pitcher that poured out silver light.

When I finished, my customer put money on the table. "For you," he said. "And thank you."

It was a bigger tip than I'd seen since I'd been in Globe, and I knew he was remembering what I'd said.

"Please. No." I pushed the money away. "It was awful, what I said. Bad mannered. I don't want your money, and I apologize."

"None needed." He shuffled the bills absently, then met my eyes. "Would you take some advice instead?"

"About what?"

"Your friend's claim."

"Joe?"

He nodded, but said nothing.

"What about him?" I sat down on the bench ready to listen.

"I couldn't help overhearing your conversation." He smiled and looked around at the tables so close together there was no hope of privacy. "And I don't think it would be wise to risk your savings on that claim of his."

In spite of myself, I felt a tremor of anger. Who was this stranger that I should listen to him?

He read my feelings and leaned toward me. "I'm a mining man. It's my job to know where the ore is, and I do know. Just like I know the claim he's working is worthless."

I didn't want to believe him. What I wanted was to be rich, to find buried treasure like in the romantic novels, and live in a mansion with many rooms and fancy wallpaper, the sound of my children's feet loud on the stairs. For all that I'd been through, I was still that silly girl who believed in fairy tales.

"Who are you?" I asked, needing a name as proof of something.

"Cal Jameson. And I live near here when I'm not on the road."

"Looking for treasure." I was mocking him, but he took me seriously.

"You might call it that."

"Are you coming or going?" It seemed important to know.

"Going. I'm just about finished here and leaving for Cananea."

That name meant nothing to me, but that fact that he was leaving made me feel as if I'd been grasping at straws and stood empty-handed.

"Then I won't see you again?" I asked.

He smiled, and the moon seemed to take on light, and I noticed for the first time that there were moths dancing around the lanterns on the tables, dancing and singeing their wings.

"I'll be here a few days yet."

"Then I'll sing for you tomorrow."

"I'll look forward to it."

He got up, bowed, and strode off along the narrow path toward town. I watched until the darkness took him.

Chapter Nineteen

Joe was back the next morning before the coffee in the big enamel pot had finished boiling. I'd lain awake a long time, thinking about what Cal Jameson had said, and had decided he was right. Still, there was a bond between Joe and me. What to do?

I gave him two extra eggs and a large helping of bacon. "Twenty dollars," I said. "That's all I can lend you."

He mopped up his egg with a hunk of bread. "Beggars can't be choosers."

"I've got to think about my babies."

He stopped chewing. "What babies?"

"I have two. They're in Ohio with my mother."

"A hell of a mother you are," he said. "Why ain't you back there with them? And where's their daddy? Or don't you know?"

"Don't you talk to me like that!" Suddenly I was crying.

"Shit!" Like most men, Joe was horrified by tears, reduced to cussing.

"Take your money!" I shoved the twenty dollars at him. "Go on! Only don't forget where it came from."

"Aw, Pete," he mumbled, but I was too far gone in my own misery to pay him any mind.

I got up and walked around the corner of the tent and ran smack into Cal Jameson.

He put out his hands to steady me. "Are you hurt? What's the matter?"

It was the feel of him, solid, warm, that shook me. "Nothing," I got out. "Everything," and leaned against him without shame.

"Tell me." He pulled out a handkerchief and, without asking permission, wiped my face.

Between sobs, I told the whole story. He said nothing, just listened, and, when I'd finished, he said: "Poor girl. What a load you've been carrying."

"I'm tired." It seemed like I'd been fighting as long as I could remember, and all so I could stand here outside this tent and cry on Jameson's shoulder.

"Stay here a minute."

I sat, too discouraged to disobey.

When he came back, he said: "You have the day off. What would you like to do?"

I couldn't think, just shook my head.

"Come on, then. Let's go for a drive. Then I'll take you to lunch, and you can sit and be waited on for a change."

He meant it! I looked down at my calico skirt and old shoes, the white apron that hadn't been washed for a week. "Wait," I said. "Please."

He understood. Cal was a man thoroughly considerate of women.

Inside the shack, I washed my face and re-did my hair, difficult because I was shaking — with excitement, with the breathlessness that comes with possibility. I put on a fresh shirtwaist and a walking skirt of deep red gabardine, and the best boots I had. Then, smiling, I went to meet him.

He had a horse and buggy hitched beside the road, and at sight of them I laughed. "You planned this!"

"Sort of." He helped me in, picked up the hitch, and got in beside me. "Where would you like to go?"

The weather was glorious, the sky dotted with small white clouds that threw purple shadows onto the mountain slopes.

101

"Anywhere," I said. "You choose."

We headed out of town and then turned west. The horse was fresh and trotted smoothly on a road cut between steep hills. The yucca was in bloom, tall torches of white flowers, and everywhere I looked I saw the golden showers of the paloverde trees.

"I love this country," I exclaimed. "It's not desert at all. Not with flowers like this."

"And not if you take the time to appreciate it," he added. "Most people don't."

"I'm glad. All the more for the rest of us."

He grinned at that. "There's plenty of room. Don't worry about being overrun with people. And especially not where we're going."

"Tell me." I clutched the side of the buggy as we swung onto a narrow trace made almost invisible by blowing grass.

"My house," he said. "I needed to check it before I left and thought you'd like to see it."

We crossed a shallow stream, then drove through a thicket of paloverdes, their green branches and yellow blossoms making a canopy overhead. Looking up, I wished I could gather a bouquet and take it back with me, the fragrance, the delicacy of twigs and flowers, and the humming of bees. There was so much beauty in the world, enough to balance the ugliness and even, perhaps, tip the scales. But you had to be aware, to "take the time" as Cal had said. I sighed to myself, a deep sigh of total content.

Cal pulled up in front of a small house. "Here we are."

I saw a porch, a yard, the glossy leaves of citrus trees brushing the roof. I saw a place where people could live and shut out the harshness of the world, and I sat there bemused, lost in a daydream.

"Come on." Cal held out his hand, and I took it, noticing

its strength and the hardness of his palm.

Inside, there were four rooms, curtains on the windows, hardwood floors carefully fitted together, and behind, across a dog-trot, another, larger room.

"My boys bunked here when they got old enough to want a room for themselves," he said, and my happiness vanished.

Of course, he had a family. And a wife somewhere. What had I been thinking? That he belonged to me? That this snug house was mine?

"Boys?" I said timidly.

"Two sons."

"And . . . and your wife?"

He swallowed hard. "She died two years ago."

"Oh." It wasn't right that I should be happy in the face of another's grief. I said: "I'm sorry."

"Life goes on. For a while I didn't want to stay here. Too many memories. So I went to work. Now . . . well, as I said, life goes on. Sometimes it even gets better."

The light was back in his eyes, and I was glad.

"Your sons? Where are they?"

"In Phoenix with my brother and his wife. They're nearly grown. Finishing up with school."

I thought of Emma and Little Joe, so far away. My sorrow must have shown on my face.

"You miss your children," he said.

"Soon I'll have enough saved to send for them." Brave words, but I believed.

"Can I help?" he asked, concern furrowing his brow. "Lend you money?"

It was one of those turning points. If I'd said yes, everything might have been different. But I was proud. And cautious, not wanting to be in his, or any man's, debt, wary of being owned. So I shook my head. "I'll manage. But thank you. No one's ever cared enough to offer."

He ran his hand over the surface of a wooden table, leaving finger marks in the dust. "Well," he said, "the offer stands. I'm leaving for Mexico. Probably be gone at least a year. But maybe . . . when I get back. . . ." His voice trailed off like the dust motes that danced in a beam of sunlight.

"Maybe," I agreed, looking around the little house and seeing it with a woman's eye. New curtains, a good scrubbing, and it would be a happy place again, watched over by the hills, the creek, the dancing branches of the paloverdes. It was a dream, but dreams, as I knew, had a way of turning into nightmares in a split second. I turned on my heel.

"Can I pick some flowers before we go?"

"If you can find any that don't have thorns."

I didn't care about thorns, or the fact that, when I got back, I had nothing but a bucket to use as a vase. I wanted only to extend the day by a few more hours, to wake in the morning and see a cloud of gold, and recall the too short time spent with a man who wanted nothing but my company, and had gone to some lengths to make that possible. Just my luck, he was leaving. But he'd be back. There was always that slim hope to hold onto.

We had a happy lunch in town. Cal had been right. It was a treat to be served instead of doing it all myself. And on the way back we drove up onto one of the hills overlooking Pinal Creek. Stone foundations and shards of pottery marked the ruins of a long-gone race, and the wind blew softly over it all.

"May I write to you?" he asked.

"I'd like that," I said. Letters would be something tangible to keep.

I put my hand on a crumbling wall. The stones were warm from the sun, and I thought of those who had loved and died there and left a mark. Perhaps letters would be all that I left. But how could I know?

"I'd like that very much."

At first Cal's letters came regularly — colorful descriptions of Mexico, its people, food, geography, and his endless curiosity about what lay beneath its ground. These weren't love letters, at least not in the accepted sense, but they did establish a kind of understanding between us, and I kept them all, tied with a piece of ribbon, in my trunk.

With the arrival of each, Harry grew happier, more certain that a romance was blossoming through the mail.

"He make good husband," he'd say. "You write back nice things."

"I always do."

"When he come home? I cook special for him."

"Not for a while." I sighed, reading over the most recent letter. "He says he's going south into Mexico to look over some old mines for somebody named Greene."

Harry shook his head. "Not good. Dangerous. Mexico very bad place."

But I had no influence over what Cal did with his life. The fragile connecting thread of our correspondence was just that — fragile — a link between two strangers who were, gradually and at a distance, enlarging a friendship.

About Joe, Harry had nothing good to say. "Why you give him money? Food? He no good for you, missy."

"He saved my life once."

"So." In Harry's eyes that was a debt of honor. "All right. Feed. But no money. You keep money."

But none of his words or my thrift mattered. By the end of that year I was broke and homeless again, and all because of an act of nature, one of those happenings that suggested I had been born unlucky and that my life would never change.

Chapter Twenty

It was a Sunday, my day off, and I'd promised Joe I'd go out to the mine. I was actually looking forward to it, and had packed a picnic lunch. He came for me in a rickety buckboard pulled by a scrawny red mule with a wicked eye.

"Just dropped off some rocks at the assay office," he said, helping me up on the splintered seat. "This might be it."

My heart leaped, he sounded so sure. "You really think?"

"There's a good chance, or my name ain't Joe Boot." He flapped the reins, and the mule moved off slowly, head down, feet dragging.

"First thing, you'd better get another mule," I said. "This one's half dead."

"Naw. He's just in a sulk. Sunday's his day off usually."

We headed in a direction opposed to the rest of the mines and diggings, and I was apprehensive.

"You're out here?" I exclaimed. "There's nothing out here."

He turned and grinned. "Hell, you got to have some brains in this business. Why dig where everybody else is?"

How could I know? The strategies of prospecting were beyond me. I trusted him. What he said made sense to me who knew nothing about faults, layers, the old, old structures of earth made before my time, or anyone's, and lying there, waiting for the pick and shovel, the sharp eyes of men who knew the secrets of the desert, the mountains, the history that paid out fortunes to so many. What I knew was that gold, silver, copper, and the thrill of discovery had brought more men West than all the cattle ranches ever had. And Joe and I were no exception. We were simply two of the tens of thousands who believed in the strike to end all strikes and the life of ease after.

But when I saw Joe's diggings, I felt as if I'd been shot in the heart.

"This?" I screamed, and I remember my voice spun away in the wind like the screech of a hawk. "This is why I lent you money?"

I stood there, looking at his shack, tin-roofed, sorry as a chicken coop, at the hole dug into the side of a crumbling hill, the pathetic pile of tailings, spilling out.

"Hey!" he said. "Hey! I've done what I could. And the stuff's here. That's a promise."

I pushed in the door of the cabin, saw a dirt floor, filthy blankets piled in a corner, unwashed pots and plates in a bucket, and I turned and said the first words that came to mind.

"You live like a hog. If your claim's as sorry as this, we're both in trouble."

He began: "Now, Pete. . . ."

But I was disgusted. "Don't you 'now, Pete' me. Don't you dare even talk to me. This place is a disgrace. No wonder people warned me about you."

"Who?" He was mad. His eyes narrowed to slits. "Who's been talking?"

"Everybody."

"God damn them!" He punched the air like it was a human face. "God damn! I'm onto something."

For the first time I was frightened of him, the fury of his expression, the hatred with which his fist had lashed out into space.

"Joe," I said. "Joe."

He blinked, focused on me. "What?"

"Let's eat." I got busy, laying out plates and food, hoping hunger would get the better of his rage.

He squatted down beside me. "Does the Chink know?" he asked.

"Know what?"

"That you're stealing off him."

"I'm not," I said, irritated at his slang. "He let me take what I wanted."

"He in love with you?"

At that I banged down my plate. "Don't be disgusting!"

He grinned, showing brown teeth. "That's what they're saying."

"Who?"

"Everybody."

"Then everybody's wrong. I work for him. That's all."

"And they're wrong about my claim, too."

We were back to that. I stared at him, silhouetted against a giant thundercloud that rose up from the mountains.

"It's going to rain," I said, changing the subject. "Maybe we should head back." The sound of thunder reached us, low and ominous. "If we leave now, we can beat the storm."

But we did not. Before we'd gone a mile, the rain hit us. We fought our way across washes, axle deep in muddy water, and on the last, steep hill into town we got out and walked ahead of the mule, slipping in muck, drenched, our clothes sticking to us. My teeth were chattering as much from fear as from cold as we stopped and looked down at the destruction. I knew what we would find, knew it as I peered through the dense curtain of rain and the hail stones that stung my face and clattered into the wagon bed. Pinal Creek had become a monster, overflowing its banks and taking houses, animals, people with it. One of those people was Harry Hu, and his wagon, shack, tables, tent, my trunk and savings were all swept away by the violence of the flood.

Joe and I stood and stared at the madness of the water, at the corpses of chickens, the trunks of trees, and once, a body, its arm raised as if pleading for rescue. I couldn't speak, couldn't breathe, simply sat down on the hill and watched in disbelief. I think I said: "Harry."

And Joe said: "Maybe he got out. We'll go look."

But I knew. Sitting there above the roar of the water, I knew. Once again I was alone, penniless, and the old man I'd loved like a father for his wisdom, his kindness, his grace was gone.

They found his body out on the flats a few days later. The wagon and my possessions were never found, or maybe they were dug up years later by kids, playing at pirates. Maybe they also found the photograph of Harry's wife, the woman with the sorrowful eyes who waited, patiently and without complaint, for the return of the husband she barely knew.

I made Joe drive me out to Gilbert's farm. His crops had been ruined, his cousin was dead, but he was planning to begin again as he had done so many times before. He and I stood awkwardly in the mud outside his cabin and looked at each other sadly, neither of us knowing how to express our feelings because language — or the lack of it — stood in our way.

Finally he said: "You be all right? You have place to go?"

I think he would have taken me in, much as his cousin had, out of that kindness the likes of which I had never known. At that moment I missed Harry with a sadness that would probably remain for the rest of my life. But I couldn't burden Gilbert with my problems, or give rise to any more vicious gossip, so I nodded and forced a weak smile. "I'll be fine," I said, not meeting his eyes. Then I turned and, planting my feet carefully in the muck and débris that was all that was left from disaster, went back to Joe who was waiting for me.

"Now what?" he wanted to know.

I was sick inside, sore from sleeping in the wagon as I'd done for the last two days. Most of the roads had been washed out, so we'd camped in an empty lot and survived as best we could. I fumbled in my purse for the bottle of laudanum. At least, I could deaden physical pain.

"What's that stuff?" he asked.

"Medicine."

"You better watch how much you take."

At that, tears came. "It doesn't matter."

He flapped the reins. "Crap! You're alive, ain't you? And in better shape than the first time I saw you. You got any money at all?"

I had ten dollars tucked in my purse along with my precious medicine.

When he heard that, his mood changed. "Well, hey! We'll get some supplies and you can come out to the claim. You own a piece, you might as well help dig."

"And live like a hog in that shack of yours."

He shot me a look. "You got a better idea?"

The trouble was, I didn't. "I want my babies," I said.

"You want it all, that's your problem. You could be back there right now, bein' a lady, but no. Not you. You'd rather sit here, feeling sorry for yourself and drinking dope."

"I'd rather be in jail than back there," I said, and meant it.

"You wouldn't. Take it from me."

I looked up at him. "Have you been in jail?"

"None of your business."

"I have a right to know who my partner is."

"And you been out here long enough to know you don't ask a man where he's been or what he's done. What if somebody asked you that . . . *Pete?*"

He was right. You took people as you found them and hoped you'd made the right choice. I looked out toward the south where the land fell away in mesas and ridges and the limestone crags of the San Carlos Reservation. The Gila River flowed there, its banks shaded by cottonwoods, its source hidden in the mountains of New Mexico that were touched by the sun and lay golden and dreaming. And there seemed to me to be hope in the fact that the earth lay unchanged, had been as it was for thousands of years. I couldn't know what lay buried in the hollows and cañons of the mountains, or in Joe's tiny plot of earth, but I could keep on, as I'd been doing most of my life, looking to the future, fighting for myself and my life.

Joe broke into my reverie. "A couple more months. We're close. You got to believe."

I took a deep breath. "All right. I'll come."

"Sooner or later, our luck's going to change."

It did that all right. It went from bad to worse.

Chapter Twenty-One

What I learned those months I was at the claim was the simple fact that to stay alive takes money. Eating, sleeping, keeping warm, working all require money, and neither Joe nor I had any.

"We're a pair of fools," I said to him over the remains of the meal I'd cooked — our last handful of beans and a rabbit Joe had shot.

He didn't answer. I thought maybe he was beginning to understand how desperate our situation was.

"We're going to starve out here, and for what?" I went on. Like everybody else, I knew about those prospectors driven mad by dreams of a strike, men who wandered the deserts, the mountains, year in and year out, and whose bones lay bleaching in the sun or buried in the graves they'd dug with their own hands. The way it looked to me, we were no better. Soon it would be our bones scattered among the rocks, our lives that were stamped out. We were, to put it plainly, committing suicide.

"You take me into town," I said finally. "I'm going to get a job."

Joe raised his head. "Doing what?"

"Anything. I'm not helpless. But I will be, if I don't get something decent to eat."

A letter from Cal would have raised my spirits. But I hadn't heard from him in months. Bleakly, I decided that Harry had been right, that he'd died somewhere in the Mexican jungle, or been captured and sold into slavery on one of the big plantations, and whatever hopes I had were better forgotten. All in all, that day was a miserable one. It was bitter cold, and the wind that whipped off the plateau tasted like ice and felt like it, too, penetrating my worn-out shawl and threadbare skirt, the only clothes I owned.

In spite of the weather, Globe was in a festive mood. The Gila Valley and Northern Railroad had been completed, and the first train, carrying the company's president, William Garland, was due in at any moment. There were bonfires burning near the station, flags and bunting decorating the store fronts, and from somewhere came the sound of a brass band, warming up. No one was interested in the plight of a small, half-frozen woman who needed work and who trudged through the crowd of revelers, determined to find it.

"Come back some other time," I was told. And: "Sorry, not today." In desperation, I even tried a few of the saloons, hoping my appearance wouldn't matter, but, of course, it did. No saloonkeeper in his right mind wanted a ragged scarecrow as an advertisement, but one of them, Bill McNelly, sat me down in the back and poured me a cup of coffee.

"Can't have you faintin' on the street," he said. "Drink up, and go on home before you get knocked down."

"I really *can* sing," I murmured, hoping he'd have second thoughts.

But he shook his head sadly. "'Twouldn't matter if you sang like Jenny Lind. It's looks that count in this business, as you must know."

I drained the mug and stood up, wanting to hate him but grateful for the coffee and his kindness.

"Thank you . . . for the drink and the advice," I said, sounding bitter in spite of myself. Then I marched out into the gathering darkness of the winter afternoon.

Most of the businesses had closed early, and it was, if

113

possible, colder than before. I trudged up the hill toward a long, low structure with a sign that read simply **Lodging**. By the time I reached the shelter of the porch and knocked on the door, my teeth were chattering.

The woman who came was tall and gaunt, like a broomstick upended. "Lord, child," she said, seeing me. "Get in this house and get warm."

She took me down a hall and into the kitchen where another woman stood over a stove and turned to stare at us, a wooden spoon like a sword in her hand.

"What on earth!" she said.

"Poor thing's near froze," said my rescuer, shoving me into a chair. "Froze and hungry, probably. Where'd you come from?" She'd addressed me, but I wasn't in any condition to answer.

"All right. Set. Get warm," she said, pressing my shoulders with heavy hands.

They fed me soup out of the big kettle and bread, and coffee laced with cream, and I ate like the starving creature I was, without stopping, until the bowl was clean, the cup empty. Then, half asleep from the food and the heat of the stove, I answered her questions.

When I finished, Lottie, the one with hair like broomstraw, folded her arms. "I reckon there's enough to do around here," she said. "What with all these men tramping in dirt, and if you ain't fussy. But two dollars a week and meals is all I can pay."

It was the meals that made me nod my head. I'd be fed, and Joe could take the money and keep on digging. "I'll do whatever you want," I said, I believe, just before I fell asleep at the kitchen table.

The snow began that night, burying the streets, the newly laid tracks, and the locomotive that had been ready to make

114

its return trip. Everyone was stranded, but the party mood had taken over the whole town. Children were sliding down the hills on makeshift sleds, and men and women were out with shovels, brooms, whatever came to hand, flinging the snow into piles higher than my head. I fought my way through the drifts to the livery to find Joe and tell him about my arrangement.

"The money's yours," I said. "Just come in and get it every week."

He grabbed my hands and did a kind of dance in the snow that was up to his knees. "You're a damn' fine partner," he said, panting from the effort. "Yesiree."

When I got back to Lottie's, I borrowed a pencil and a piece of paper and wrote a letter to my mother, telling her I was now running a boarding house and would soon have enough money to come home. Why did I lie? Maybe to convince myself, or maybe I simply couldn't admit to defeat. Not then.

Chapter Twenty-Two

Lottie's boarding house burned to the ground on the May afternoon when the telegram reached me. She and I stood helplessly in the street and watched as the fire raged, and black smoke drew a curtain across the sky.

Tears ran down her cheeks that were streaked with soot. "Everything I owned," she mumbled. "Every damn' thing."

In the few months I'd been with her I'd learned her story, one of simple determination and hard work. She and her husband had come West, hoping the dry climate would be good for his lungs. Together they'd put all their money into the house. And then the husband died, leaving Lottie to succeed or fail. Now all her scrimping, all her labor was turning to ashes, along with the belongings of her boarders and the few things that were mine. I put my arms around her, but was helpless to console her for the loss, and suddenly I was crying, too. No matter how hard I tried, or what I did, I seemed always to find myself facing a blank wall.

And then Ruby, who worked in the kitchen, came running, sweating and red-faced, up the hill toward us. "Oh, Lord," she kept saying, "oh, Lord, what're we going to do?" which didn't help.

"For heaven's sake, hush!" I said, but my words were drowned out by the arrival of the fire wagon, too late. The roof fell in with a crash, spattering sparks that threatened the neighboring structures and caused us to move farther down the road.

Suddenly Ruby began digging in her market basket. She'd

gone shopping, as she always did, and at the sight of the vegetables and meat, useless without even a pot to cook them in, Lottie and I cried harder.

"Telegram!" Ruby said breathlessly. "They gave it to me, 'cause I was headed up here."

When at last she found it and handed it over, crumpled, stained with blood that had leaked from the meat, I wanted to throw it away and run, run until my legs gave out, and my lungs collapsed. Telegrams meant disaster. I held the envelope as if it were a rattlesnake, and my hand shook like an aspen leaf.

"Open it!" Ruby demanded, curiosity overcoming her horror at the fire.

"I can't." Pictures flew through my mind — Emma, Little Joe laid out like angels in small coffins, calling for me in despair. The world was a pit opening at my feet, a hole in the ground from which there was no escaping. But at last I ripped the seal and read the message that marked me, changed me, left me a fugitive, a fallen woman forever.

Mother dying. Children ill. Come at once.

There was a rock on my back that kept me from moving, and a blackness in front of my eyes. There was a buzzing in my ears, as if a swarm of bees surrounded me. There was the fire, red tongues whipped by a sudden wind that blew sparks that lit on my arms, burned holes in my skirt, and I unable to help myself or even to speak. I remember I put out my hands, as if I was holding off another blow, and Lottie, in spite of her troubles, grabbed them.

"What is it? What, child?"

I had no words, simply handed her the telegram. She read it and looked at me, defeat in her eyes. "What'll you do?" she asked, as if I had answers.

One thing I did know. I was going home if I had to walk every mile. I wasn't thinking, only feeling. I didn't think until later when there was nothing left to do but think — and regret my hasty action.

"I'm going home," I said. "Home." And with the words spoken at last I turned and ran, leaving the holocaust, the women, the fire fighters open-mouthed behind me.

Chapter Twenty-Three

Joe's plan was madness, and I was mad to agree to it. But desperation and poverty do strange things to a person. For a few hours I stopped thinking and latched onto his wild scheme as if it were a lifeline. He made it sound easy, and I believed. We would hold up the stage in Cane Springs Cañon where the road took a bend before it descended to the little settlement of Troy near the San Pedro River. Travelers always carried cash. We'd rob them and ride south to Benson where I would get on the train and head home. It sounded so simple when he said it, but, then, talk is always easier than the doing.

Joe stole two horses for us. I hacked off my hair and took a pair of pants and a shirt off a miner's clothesline. And then I was Pete again, my pants held up with a piece of rope, my feet blistered in the boots I'd also stolen — too large, but thieves can't be choosy.

The sky was that washed-out blue it turns before the summer rains. Along the base of the mountains was a haze, half dust, half heat waves, and somewhere off in the brush a cicada buzzed. Otherwise, the land was still as if it were holding its breath, as if it were waiting, like I was, for the sound of hoofs, the signal for action. Suddenly I was scared. What was I doing there in the stillness, my heart thumping in my breast? How had I fallen so far from grace? I was Pearl Hart, raised as a lady, and I was about to take a pistol in my hand and use it to commit a crime. And there was my partner, grinning at me as if it were all a game, a lark, an everyday occurrence.

"Loosen up," he said suddenly. "This ain't the time for female hysterics."

"Let's go back." My jaws and throat ached from holding in tears. "Let's forget it. I changed my mind."

His smile vanished, and he put his hands on my shoulders. They were big hands, hard from shoveling rocks and sand. "And then what?" he wanted to know. "Then we'll starve, and you'll go crazy over those kids, and it'll be my fault." He gave me a shake.

"But . . . ?"

"But nothing. They'll get us for horse stealing no matter what, so you're over your head already."

The truth of his words sank in. It was too late. For me it had always been too late. If I got out of this, if I got home, I'd never leave it again.

"Please, God . . . ," I started to pray as I hadn't prayed in years, but even that plea came too late.

I heard the sound of hoofs, the jingling of traces, and Joe looked at me out of narrowed eyes.

"You going to chicken out?"

I wiped my nose on my sleeve, not caring how it appeared. "I'll be all right." My voice came out in a croak.

"You better be. This ain't no game." He pulled down the brim of his hat. I could smell his sweat and my own. To me it smelled of fear and all the poverty of the last ten years. I gritted my teeth. Never again! I was never going to be poor again!

And then the horses came around the bend, and I stepped out in front of them and fired into the air. I can see it still — the terrified animals, their yellow teeth in open jaws, how they plunged and squatted down on lathered haunches as the driver hauled on the reins.

"Toss down your pistol. Then keep your hands where I can

120

see 'em." Joe sounded menacing, and the driver obeyed fast.

"Everybody out," came the next order.

It seemed Joe had been born to be a road agent, as if he'd done this many times before — and I wondered if I knew him at all, this man in whose hands I'd placed my future. But I didn't have time to wonder much.

"Stop gaping!" he snapped at me. "Get them to hand over what they've got."

He gestured at the three men who were coming slowly out of the coach, their hands in the air, and my heart sank as I recognized the last one. Gilbert Hu was staring at me as if he thought his life was over.

"Oh, God," I said, hesitating.

Joe lost his patience. "Hurry up! We don't have all day!"

I pulled the brim of my hat down low. Why hadn't we thought about masks? Why hadn't we thought about the consequences if we were identified and caught? But, once again, it was too late for me. I was in it — and I'd get out. Somehow.

"You heard him," I said, trying to disguise my voice. "Put your money in the sack. And no tricks."

They did what they were told, so frightened their hands trembled. Except for Gilbert. He dropped his money purse into the sack and looked straight at me. Then he said two words: "Please, missy."

"Shut up!" I stepped away from his all-seeing stare as memories came at me. Harry serving me bowls of soup, Gilbert offering me shelter when he had none for himself. I wanted to cry then, for all of us — Harry, Gilbert, their wives somewhere in China, waiting, waiting, as so many women did — waiting until their hearts gave out and with nothing to show for their patience.

As I hesitated, Joe yelled: "Jesus! Come on, we can't stand here all day."

121

I reached into the bag and pulled out a handful of bills and coins and tossed them on the ground. "Here," I said. "So you won't be flat broke."

Then I ran, breaking stride just long enough to grab the driver's pistol where it lay at the side of the road.

"Smart girl," Joe said, throwing me the reins of one of the horses, a bony old mare with a mind of her own.

She wanted to go back where she belonged, and I was never a good horsewoman. When I climbed into the saddle, she took off at a lope back to town and the stable. I was alone in the brush, fighting a creature as determined as I was. Sweat poured into my eyes and blinded me as I tried to get the animal to obey. She was strong and getting mad. I could feel her anger through the saddle leather, see it in her laid-back ears. If she bucked, I'd go off and land in the rocks where the buzzards would find me before the law did.

"Where the hell you going?" Joe burst out of the brush and grabbed a rein.

"I can't get her to listen."

"She damn' well better." He headed off, pulling me with him.

I held onto the horn as we moved off at a lunging trot. I'd lost my hat; the sun burned through my hair to my scalp. My face was bleeding from the whiplash of thorny mesquite and catclaw branches. It seemed that, for a long time, we looked for the trail that would take us south. Then I recognized a pile of rock I'd seen before.

"You damn' fool!" I yelled at Joe. "We're going in circles."

He slowed and looked back at me, and I saw a kind of panic in his eyes. I snatched the reins and pulled up the mare.

"Can't you tell what direction south is?" I was still yelling, furious that I was depending on this man who didn't know his directions, who I'd trusted with my life. Below us the sun reflected off the river, but the western mountains were already in the shadow of afternoon. "Come on, and let's get out of here," I said, forcing the mare past him down a rough trail. Strangely, with my determination, she obeyed me, and, leading the way, I rode fast down the valley of the San Pedro River, going for broke like the criminal I was.

Chapter Twenty-Four

It's not an easy trip, that game trail south out of Cane Springs. That's brush country. And rock. Miles of rock that wears down a horse's feet and drives the rider crazy with the need to go carefully. There are holes and dry washes where you don't expect them, so that suddenly your horse jumps off a level plain into sand up to its hocks and flounders with you holding on for dear life. And there's the brush — thorny mesquite — the branches clawing at you, raking you raw, and the blaze of ocotillo flowers hiding more thorns beneath their beauty, all laying a trap, waiting for the unwary.

You push and you push, and the night isn't much cooler than the day has been. The horses are dragging, and you ache in places you never thought of, but you keep going because you know they're behind you, on your trail, and you're running for your life and the lives of your children. That's how it is, see? You've done this thing, done it and be damned, and you're reaching for freedom like always, only this time it's everybody's freedom, not just your own. It's Joe's, and your mother's, and those babies'. It's the mare under you who's moving slower now, whose sweat mingles with your own, who needs a rest as badly as you do, maybe more.

You can feel her heart struggling under your legs. She's a tough old girl, but she's done as much as she can, and you feel like she's part of you. She's got courage — more than you ever had. And strength. And as her strength falters, you feel your own body crying out. For water. For a chance to stop and breathe the hot night air without the need to keep moving.

You want to lie down and look at the stars that splash like a billion diamonds on the dark sky. You want to forget what you've done, to close your eyes and be a girl again, cared for, laughing, the world at your feet. You want it back, your life before you gave it away for the sake of dreams. You want. You want. And at last you call out: "Stop!"

And Joe turns around, the whites of his eyes gleaming in the dark. "Not yet," he says. "Not yet."

"Now." I slump in the saddle. "Now."

Above us the sky moves, and the stars. The world spins. We move across the earth like ants — tiny, helpless. Small. So small. So close to nothingness. Over and over I've lived that journey. It haunts my dreams, my days. If only. . . . If only. . . . That's what I say to myself. If only I hadn't been human, so exhausted that I fell from the saddle and lay on the ground like a corpse, and all the while the posse coming closer, set on capturing a pair of fools.

There was a drought that year. The river was low, hardly a trickle, and the grass only withered yellow stems. No energy there for tired horses that cropped the leaves of the mesquite after drinking from the slime that passed for water.

We didn't make a fire. We didn't want to be seen, and there was always the danger of starting a bigger one. So we lay on the sand, drinking from the canteen, chewing jerky, and smoking a cigarette or two. I must have slept finally, because, when I opened my eyes, the stars were fading, and the light around us was pale, like smoke or fog, and my clothes were damp from dew.

"What time is it?" I asked.

"Time to move out." Joe was studying the sky.

"Not yet." I felt old, unable to move.

"Pretty soon, then." He lit a cigarette, and the smell of the match, of the tobacco, was sharp in the morning air.

"How much did we get?" I wanted to know. I reached for the sack that lay between us.

"Might as well count it," he said. "Probably more'n enough to get you out."

There was almost four hundred dollars, what seemed a fortune. I split it into two piles.

"Half is yours."

He shook his head. "You'll need it more'n me. I'm aiming to sell these horses, get me some clothes, and head back."

"To Globe?" I was astonished.

"Why not?"

"They might get you."

He shook his head. "Naw. I'll be back diggin', without them knowing I was ever gone. Don't you worry."

But I was worried. Something kept nagging at me. Something left undone. I sat and replayed the hold-up in my mind, while the sky in the east turned yellow, the color of lemons, and the mountains in the west grew red like embers in an old fire.

"Gilbert Hu knew it was me," I said at last. "He called me 'missy.'"

"Well, he don't know me from Adam," came Joe's reply. "Besides, who's going to believe a Chinaman?"

"Some people just might." I sat, still struggling for the missing piece of the puzzle. When I remembered, my stomach seemed to turn over. It took a minute before I could speak again. "We never cut the traces," I whispered. "They were all back in town while we were riding in circles." *Thanks to you,* I thought.

He stared at me a minute, then jumped to his feet. "God damn us for a pair of fools. Let's get out of here!"

That day was worse than the first. We rode along the river

with its scum of water, its treacherous quicksand, our flight slowed by the mesquite forest that grew, like the forest in a fairy tale, without a visible trail. Sometimes we got off and led the horses, pushing our way through, fighting off flies and midges that whined around our faces, biting, stinging, landing in our eyes so we had to stop, blinking and cursing and nearly blind. And always the knowledge that behind us was a posse, closer than we'd thought.

Home! It was the memory of home that kept me going. I promised myself that, if I ever got back to my mother's house, I'd never leave. I'd become the dutiful daughter, the good mother, the lady I'd been brought up to be.

My feet were blistered, my body ached, I itched from a thousand insect bites, but I went on. Not talking. It took all my strength to move. Long after dark we rode into a clearing and found the empty house. It looked like a haven — four walls, a roof, a place to lie down and rest.

"Let's stop." I was whispering as if there were ears to hear, men crouched in the brush, hidden by darkness.

Joe looked around. Listened. We heard nothing but the fluting call of night hawks, the shrilling of crickets. He helped me dismount and kept one arm around me while I staggered to the door, my feet and legs too numb to support me or even feel pain.

"Wait," he cautioned. "This is just the place for a rattler or two to hole up."

He went inside and struck a match. It made a tiny glow against the dark before it went out and left the night blacker than before. He struck another. I could see him moving around, checking the rafters, the corners. At last he said: "Come on in."

I sat down with a groan. "How far to Benson?"

"Maybe ten miles." He was standing in the doorway, his

127

body black against the starlight.

"We can get there tomorrow, then."

"Yep." He turned and looked out the way we'd come. "This time tomorrow night you'll be on that train. Right now, you get some sleep. I'll keep watch."

It was the last thing I heard. I lay down on the hard dirt floor and closed my eyes. I don't know what woke me, maybe a horseshoe ringing on stone, or the nicker of the mare, but I was wide awake in a split second and watching the open door.

Beside me, Joe lay snoring. *Keeping watch, indeed!* I thought. I was reaching for the pistol that lay by his side when Sheriff Bill Truman's body blocked the pale light that shone in the door.

"Stop right there and you won't get hurt," he said.

My hopes, my fears exploded into rage, and I went for him like a wildcat, fingers and teeth and a kick aimed at his groin. Ten miles! Ten lousy miles were all that lay between me and my dream, and Joe asleep like the dead. I was screaming, incoherent, fighting, but for all of that I might have been a fly. Truman caught me, pinned my hands, and let his posse members take care of Joe who sat, blinking and useless as tits on a boar.

They dragged me outside still kicking, or trying to, and handcuffed me, and, when I tried to run for the brush, one of the men caught me around my knees and brought me down. I lay there in the sand and rocks, tasting blood from a split lip, along with tears of frustration. It was like being with Frank all over again — me, helpless against male strength, the power of pure muscle over my own wanting.

It had all been for nothing, those torturous days with hope, dangling like a jewel, ahead. I'd forfeited the chance to see my children by trusting Joe to get me through, to keep watch. The thought was bitter as salt. I don't know who I hated more —

the sheriff and his men, or Joe, or myself, Pearl Hart, who'd always done the wrong thing, taken the wrong road, sure that the taking was right.

I didn't say a word during the long trip back. It seemed there wasn't anything left to say.

Chapter Twenty-Five

In the Florence jail, they stripped me, gave me a bath, and produced a hideous dress with purple stripes that was too large. The final blow was a hat that looked like a pie plate. "Get that thing out of here!" I sailed the hat through the bars of my cell straight at the jailer.

He was unmoved. "There's folks want to see you. Best put it on. Act like a lady. Maybe you'll get off easy."

"Go away," I shrieked. "Go away. I don't want to see anybody."

The little jail had no provisions for women, so I was at the end of a row of cells that held men, with Joe on the opposite end. Everybody but Joe cheered and whistled at my show of spirit, but I turned on them next.

"Why don't you all shut up? I'm not in here for your amusement."

"You'll do till something better comes along, honey," one of them said, grinning.

"Our little Pearl," another called. "Our Pearl beyond price."

At that they all hooted, and I lost my temper. I rattled the bars and called for Bill Truman at the top of my lungs.

He came running, worried about a riot in his two-bit prison.

"You get me out of here," I told him. "It's not right, me in here with these animals."

They all roared at that, and started pounding on the bars.

"See? You see? Now you get me out!" I stamped my foot and winced from the pain of a festering blister. "And please, I'm begging you, find out what happened to my babies."

Truman looked down his long nose at me. "It makes a good story, Pearl," he said. "Too good, if you get my meaning. But you're being moved to Tucson tomorrow. Best pack your things." He gave a wry grin at his last words, turned, and spoke to the others. "No more racket in here. Any more and it'll go hard on you." Then he left, slamming the heavy door behind him.

They took me to Tucson under guard. I don't know how they moved Joe. We were kept apart, probably because everyone was afraid we'd plan an escape. And I was thinking about escape, about how I was going to get home. They didn't believe my story, so I was left in ignorance about the fate of my children, my imagination painting a thousand scenes of agony and death until I wanted to scream.

A few days in prison had taught me all I ever wanted to know about that life. Someone watched every move I made, like I was a dangerous animal or a crazy woman set on killing myself. I thought about that, too, about hanging myself from the rafters, or slicing my wrists. But there was still life in my veins. I was too young to die, especially by my own hand.

But if I were free, if I, somehow, made it back to Toledo and buried myself among those pale urns who were family friends, who would know? Who would connect Mrs. Pearl Hart with the rag-tag female, dressed in men's clothes, who had stuck up a stagecoach in far-away Globe? The answer, as I saw it, was no one. So I set my mind to it. The rest was easy.

In Tucson I had my own cell. I could dress and undress, relieve myself without the eyes of a bunch of prisoners following every move. Even better, I had a certain amount of freedom. Overnight I had become a celebrity. Newspapermen wanted to interview me. Journalists from popular magazines waited in line outside the jail just for the purpose of talking to me, Pearl Hart, the Bandit Queen. Did it hurt, being branded a criminal?

Of course. I was ashamed. I almost hoped my mother had died so that she would be spared the horrors of my actions. So, though I told those men all kinds of stories that they believed and printed, I was also careful to tell them the truth in hope of garnering sympathy for myself. I told them about Frank and the beatings I'd endured, and about my children. I watched them scribbling away on their tablets, and, when they had gotten the first part right, I made up the second. They believed my lies. How could they not? They had been raised on yellow journalism and tales of the wildest of Wests.

They made me pose for photographs with carefully unloaded pistols and the clothes I'd worn. They made me a heroine, although I could have told them otherwise. They hauled me in and out of my cell and never noticed that the old adobe wall was caving in and that even a blind man could've worked his way out during the night hours. I kept my knowledge to myself while I spun my yarns and tried to look sinister, holding pistols and even a shotgun at the urging of photographers.

You learn a lot in a prison cell. How to rely on yourself, and not give any secrets away. How to pass the time making plans while smiling at the jailers. How not to trust anyone else with your life. Once before I'd congratulated myself on being a quick learner. This time I was going to make sure of it.

Chapter Twenty-Six

"Damn it! Damn it!" I wanted to pound my fists into the dirt, but they were trapped under me as I lay, half in and half out of the hole I'd gouged in the wall. I could see stars, hear laughter and music from a saloon down the block. What a shock I'd give some passing drunk with my head sticking out like a gopher. In spite of my predicament, I laughed, and with the laughter felt the adobe crumble the littlest bit. There was hope for me, after all.

"Easy," I said to myself. "You'll make it." And inched forward again.

Slowly, terrified that the jailer would discover me and drag me back into prison by my heels, I hauled my way out — the longest minutes I've ever spent. When, at last, I crawled to my feet, I was dizzy and stood, taking deep breaths of the sweet desert air.

And then I was running through the narrow streets, dodging past darkened houses where people slept in innocence and safety, keeping in the shadows, like a street-wise tomcat, and always looking back over my shoulder for signs of pursuit. I was Pete again, dressed in the clothes I'd posed in for the photographers. It seemed I'd never be rid of that identity, that I'd spend the rest of my life as a vagabond youth, running, always running from someone or something that threatened my existence.

This time, though, I was on my own, and glad of it. This time there was no Joe Boot to guide me, for whatever that was worth. Alone, I found the railroad yard, stood watching, listening, hunted, all senses sharpened, my body tense, more animal than woman, more shadow than substance.

A pair of railroad dicks came down the tracks, carrying lanterns. The yellow lights looked mysterious in the darkness, like will-o'-the-wisps, or goblin lamps as we used to call them when I was a child. With the memory of childhood came sorrow. So long ago, it all seemed as if it had belonged to some other girl, one I didn't know and couldn't recognize, a wraith who believed that life was glorious. Abruptly I squared my shoulders. Feeling sorry for myself was a waste of time, and dangerous as well. I watched the men inspect the cars and move off slowly down the tracks. When they had gone, I jumped into a freight car. It felt like home.

The train headed east, back through Benson, the train I would have taken had I not trusted in Joe and allowed us to be caught. *Joe!* I spat at the thought. From here on, I vowed that I'd place my trust only in myself and never in a man.

Through the partially open door of the car I watched the country move past: dry country, drought-stricken and desolate, ringed by bare mountains that looked like waves of the sea captured and frozen in time. The land was parched, and so was I. This trip I had no provisions, no water, and my tongue felt like a wad of cotton in the cave of my mouth.

Still, I refrained from getting off when the train stopped in Benson. It was too close to Tucson, and by now they'd be looking for me. Where the next stop was, I didn't know, but I figured I could make it that far. Had to. Otherwise my escape was in vain.

On and on — the earth shriveled, the mountains, gray and dun, turning purple when an infrequent cloud formed in that unforgiving sky. I could see buzzards, their black wings stretched out in a glide as they searched for food. Creatures of death, they were, scavengers, ripping the meat from the bones of the dead.

I slept, or perhaps fainted, from heat, from thirst that scoured me from the inside out, and I only woke when the train racketed to a stop somewhere in the midst of that awful plain. I peered out, saw houses, a few trees, a hedge of oleanders bright with blossoms. Water! There had to be some. Even a horse trough would be welcome. I jumped out of the freight car and stood a minute, steadying myself, watching for trouble. Seeing no one, I went off down a street. In the backyard of a house I found a pump, stuck my head under, and let the blessed water cool me. Then I drank. And drank some more, wishing I had a canteen to fill.

Next came the problem of food. I'd have to steal it. Well, I'd stolen before. Pinching something to eat out of the store of an unwary grocer would be easier than sticking up a stage-coach. The little *tiendita* was dim and cool. Inside, a woman with a small child lingered by a basket of melons. The proprietor ignored me, probably because I looked like I couldn't afford so much as a loaf of bread. When he turned to speak to the child, I grabbed some apples — withered things, but beggars can't be choosers — and on the way out I took a handful of limes, grateful that my boy's trousers had deep pockets. Made careless by success, I headed back to the train.

How it happened, I never did know. One minute I was sauntering up the dusty street. The next, my arms were pinned from behind in a grip so tight I thought they were broken. I couldn't move, but I had the use of my tongue and burst out in a storm of words. Bad words. All the ones I'd ever heard, and I'd heard plenty in the saloons and gambling dens. I hollered and yelled, standing in that little street in Deming, and it did me no good at all. I'd been caught again, and this time I knew in my bones I'd not get free.

"Shut up, Pearl," came the advice from the man whose marshal's badge caught the sun and reflected it into my eyes. "Anything you say'll be held against you."

"I know that, cock-sucker," I said, then fell silent in shame.

Later, George Scarborough told the press I was the foulest-mouthed female he'd ever met. In his case that was probably true, but where I was headed, I met many worse.

Chapter Twenty-Seven

Joe Boot got thirty years for his part in the hold-up. Thirty years! If they gave me the same, I'd be old when I got out — old and unable to help myself. Thirty years in a cell, looking out at the living, and for nothing. We hadn't injured anyone. The money had been returned, and I was glad about that for Gilbert's sake. As I thought about my predicament, it seemed that we were being used, made an example, but only because we couldn't help ourselves. Joe had said nothing in his own defense, which was understandable. He wasn't a talker or much of a thinker, accepting life as it came.

I was cut from different cloth, and, besides, I was terrified at the thought of being locked away. The terror, however, turned to fury. How dare they do this to me? How dare they keep me from finding out what had happened at home? I'd spent my life doing time of one kind or another. When had I ever had a chance to live without having to fight for every cent, every belief, every breath? My anger was so fierce it almost consumed me before I fought it down. Control in such circumstances is hard, but I managed, and by doing so found eloquence.

I was standing in front of the all-male jury, wearing once again that hideous dress of purple stripes, and all the anger and frustration I'd ever felt poured out.

"You men . . . none of you know what it's like being a woman. Helpless. Trying to make do on your own. Cut off from your family. You only think you know.

"I didn't want this trial," I told them. "I didn't want to be judged by a court full of men, according to laws made by men. The law says, 'a jury of one's peers,' but you're not my peers. You're men, and you rule by the laws you make without even thinking about women. I was married once. To a man who beat and nearly killed me." At the memory, which seemed as fresh as yesterday, I had to fight off tears. "That's right," I went on. "He beat me. For everything. For nothing. That's why I'm here today, being judged. Because I ran away to save myself and got lost in the trying. Because I gave up my babies. But I'm a mother, and I want to know how they are. No one will tell me or even try to find out. I've been treated like a criminal because all I wanted to do was go home to them. And now I ask you to help."

I stared at each of them in turn, bearded, dour creatures who stared back at me with unreadable faces. "You wouldn't be here today without women. You were all born of a woman, nurtured, taught, loved by a woman."

I paced up and down in front of them, wanting to tear out my hair, but knowing that only logic would sway their decision. "Think about your mothers before you condemn me. Think about me, separated from my children. Think about the fairness of your laws. Women sent to jail for adultery while the men go free. Women blamed for the fact that their husbands beat them. Women who abandon their children because they can't care for them. This is justice?"

I laughed cynically into those solemn faces. "No, gentlemen, it is *not* justice. There won't be any justice until women are given a say in the making of laws to protect themselves. What I am asking you for is your compassion. Your help."

Then I sat down to wait for the verdict. The minutes ticked past, and I closed my eyes so as not to have to watch the clock. If I was set free, I promised myself, I'd never do anything foolish again. Never.

The jury reëntered the room and read the verdict.

Not guilty!

Free! I was free to go!

I hurried out of the courtroom, pushing through the crowd that had gathered, smiling at the newspaper reporters who had applauded my speech. I'd barely gone fifty yards when the sheriff caught up with me.

"Not so fast, Pearl," he said.

"Now what?" I was finished with that town and the men in it.

"You're under arrest." He took my arm.

I tried to pull away. My heart said: *Run!* My feet wouldn't move. What law had I broken? What crime had I committed by simply walking into the sunlight?

"Didn't you hear?" My voice was shrill. "I'm free. I'm not guilty."

"And the judge wasn't pleased with your act. He figured you influenced the jury, so he issued another warrant for the theft of Henry Bacon's pistol."

"Who's Bacon? I never stole any pistol."

"Yeah, you did. Bacon was driving that stage. He says you took his pistol, and there were witnesses who agree with him." He gave a tug at my arm.

"There's a mistake." I was babbling. So this is where my plea had gotten me! This was what happened to a woman simply trying to save herself! "I can't be tried again. It's against the law. The law you men made."

He grinned at me. He had brown teeth behind his stained mustache. "New case," he said. "Nobody said anything about the pistol before. Now come on to jail and no more trouble. Maybe you'll get off easy. If you keep your mouth shut . . . ," he added, as he shoved me down the street ahead of him.

But I didn't. I was sentenced to five years in Yuma Prison

139

for the theft of that damn' Forty-Five. When the sentence came down, I wept. They might as well have hanged me. Yuma Prison was two steps lower than hell.

Chapter Twenty-Eight

All across Arizona people were gathered, waiting to see me, the infamous Pearl Hart. Men, women, children gaped through the window when the train stopped for water. I could hear them. They didn't bother to whisper. It was as if I wasn't really there, or had no feelings, as if I were a life-size doll without a heart.

"That's her! That's Pearl!"

"I seen her. I did."

"She looks like anybody else."

"Ugly as sin. That comes from a wicked life."

Wicked, indeed! I stared back at the crowd on the station platform, crossing my eyes, sticking out my tongue, aping their gestures. If they wanted to see a freak in a circus, I'd give them one.

Some laughed. One child, a boy about six, screamed and buried his face in his mother's skirts.

"Shame!" she called out. "Scaring an innocent boy."

"Damn you!" I yelled back. "Damn you all!" And had the pleasure of seeing them fall back, frightened of me, of what they imagined I could do if I chose.

"They'll stick you in the snake pit in Yuma if you don't behave," the guard said.

"What's that?"

"Solitary. And dark. You stay in there till they figure you've been broke. It don't take long." He leered like a gargoyle.

"You don't scare me," I said.

"Missus High and Mighty. You'll find out about scared soon enough. When the snakes and scorpions get after you."

141

He went to the end of the car and lit a cigar, leaving me handcuffed to the arm of the seat like a circus monkey chained to a stake.

"I hate you," I whispered, too low for him to hear. "I hate all of you."

Hot wind blew through the window, and dust, and cinders. Beyond was desert, miles of it, broken only by the arms of cactus, the frail green branches of paloverde trees. And rock, lots of rock, rust-colored like old iron. Even that changed as we moved west. Rocks turned to mountains, harsh and black. Nothing grew on those slopes or peaks, not even weeds, and I tasted the beginning of despair.

For the next five years I was doomed to live in this place that might have been the desolation of the moon. For the first time in many years, I said a prayer.

"Open your mouth."

Humiliated, standing in the prison doctor's office, wearing only my underclothes, I did as I was told.

Like a mare at auction, I was being weighed, checked, looked over for defects. What I wanted to do was bite his fingers as he probed my teeth. Instead, I closed my eyes.

"A couple of loose ones," he said, stepping back. "Are you having any pain?"

The pain was in my heart, hidden from his probing. "No," I said. "No pain."

He sighed. "It's a wonder."

"It isn't when you had a husband who knocked you around."

Dr. Milton Tatum, for all his business-like manner, was kind. "I'm sorry," he said. "Tell me if they hurt, will you? We have a dentist here."

I nodded, let him weigh and measure me, ask questions

that would haunt me for the rest of my life and beyond.

"Do you smoke?"

"Yes. Cigarettes."

"Anything else I should know about?"

"Laudanum. Morphine when I can get it." I said that to shock him and succeeded.

"Are you having any difficulty?" he asked finally.

I shook my head. "I've been in jail since June. They don't pass out dope to the prisoners."

"Good girl," he said.

"Why?"

He put down his pencil and looked me straight in the eye. "Because I've had prisoners on withdrawal before. It's not pleasant. For me. Or them. Or anybody else."

"Oh," I said, trying to remember my own symptoms. "I guess I was too busy to notice."

"Then you're one of the lucky ones." He picked up the pencil. "Religion?"

"Catholic. At least I was. Once."

He pretended not to notice the tears in my eyes. "Do you drink?"

"No."

"Where'd you get those scars on your leg?"

"My husband," I said with scorn. "I already told you about him. Actually, I think he's dead, and thank God for it. Any more questions, doctor?"

He finished writing before answering. I watched him fill in the blank spaces. Hair: black. Eyes: gray. Weight: one hundred pounds. Height: five feet two inches. There I was, down on paper, except they'd left out everything important. They'd left out my life and the fact that I had scars on my heart. Now I was merely a number — 1559. My humanity had been left at the prison gate.

I swallowed the bile that threatened to choke me. "I don't think I'll last five years."

He looked up at me. "You have no choice," he said.

Chapter Twenty-Nine

Yuma Territorial Prison was built in 1876 on a bluff above the Colorado River. Its location alone was enough to strike fear into the heart of any prisoner planning to escape. The current, where the Colorado and Gila Rivers meet at the base of the prison hill, is swift and dangerous, death to all but the strongest swimmer. To the south lies Mexico and a desert of sand and lava beds, and the same desert surrounds Yuma on all other sides. It's desolate, lonely country, and it's damned hot.

My cell in the women's yard faced west. From May to November I was subject to the sun's merciless eye until it set in a mass of fiery clouds. My cell, dug into the rock of the hill, held the heat until nearly dawn when it was finally possible to sleep. Well, sleep of a sort. The prison was overrun with cockroaches, bedbugs, and the mosquitoes that bred in the backwaters of the river. I scratched myself raw most nights, and the weekly bath they allowed me wasn't enough to keep the bedbugs away. As a result, I kept my hair cut short as a man's, unflattering but easy to care for, and, in the heat, cool.

The women's yard was separated from the men's by a fence, so I had privacy, but it was unwanted. As the only female prisoner, I was alone most of the time, day and night. Oh, the people who lived in town came up to the prison to sell tobacco and fruit and candy, and many were curious about me and stopped to talk, but when they were gone, the place seemed even emptier, and I was left with only my thoughts for company.

In the mornings some of the men were taken out to work

in the fields across the river, while the rest worked in the laundry or the kitchen. I would watch them go, all dressed alike in their prison uniforms, and wonder if Joe was among them, if he could see me, my face pressed to the bars of the cell where his incompetence had put me.

I'd watch, wishing I could go with them just for an hour, just so I could talk and have an ordinary conversation with someone other than the guard who brought me my meals, let me out to walk around the yard, and brought the curious to stare at me as if I were an animal in a zoo.

One visitor, a woman, brought me a copy of *Cosmopolitan* magazine with my own story in it. I read the piece over and over, laughing at the lies I'd told and crying over the parts that were true. About Joe they quoted me as saying: "He's got no sand." I couldn't remember having said that. It was an odd phrase, one I wouldn't have chosen, even though I had lost all respect for him.

Sand. Well, there was enough of that in Yuma. Sometimes, when the wind blew hard, we'd be suffocated in sand. It got into my eyes and nose, my ears, my blankets, and piled up in the corners of the cell so deep I needed a shovel. Sand, stone, sun, solitude. There were days when I'd have killed for a drop of rain or a kind human voice.

"Why can't I eat in the dining room like all the rest?" I asked Ed Simmons, the guard. "Why do I have to stay here by myself all the time?"

He looked me up and down before he spoke. "There's two hundred and fifty men out there, and you're a woman, that's why."

"Is that my fault?"

"Nope. But it's a fact, and the super don't want no riots." He put my dinner tray on the table and eyed me again. "You lookin' for company?" he asked.

146

His meaning was plain. "Go to hell," I snapped.

"Just checking." He grinned and stepped through the metal door that he locked behind him. Then he peered back through the bars. "Let me know if you change your mind. Five years is a long time."

I picked up the bowl of stew, intending to throw it at him, but he moved off fast and left me to eat alone.

Sometimes I thought about Cal and allowed myself the luxury of dreaming about what could have been, which made me more miserable than before. Even if by some miracle he was alive, he wouldn't want me now, wouldn't look at me with that glimmer in his eyes that had touched me so. He was a gentleman. I was jail bait.

How I hated myself and my own foolishness! How dreary the days were — and the nights — with no company but the striped tomcat who showed at meals and sometimes curled up on my lap. If only to hear a voice, I sang all the songs I knew, made up others, and, when I'd run out of ideas, started over. I bit my nails and chewed on the skin around them. I even went so far as to try to build sand castles on the barren floor of the yard, squatting in the dust like a five year old, lost in an imaginary place of my own creation.

Finally, tired of all of these distractions, I asked for paper and a pencil. I'd write my memoirs, such as they were. I'd write poetry, though I'd never liked poetry or paid much attention to it. But poems were like songs. They told a story, and they rhymed, and I sat for hours, trying to achieve a line, a stanza that I liked.

My favorite went:

The sun was brightly shining on a pleasant afternoon
My partner, speaking lightly, said:
"The stage will be here soon."

We saw it coming around the bend
and called to them to halt,
And to their pockets we attended,
if they got hurt, it was their fault.

While the birds were sweetly singing,
and the men stood up in line
And the silver softly ringing
as it touched this palm of mine
Then we took away their money,
but left them enough to eat
And the men looked so funny
as they vaulted to their seat.

Then up the road we galloped,
quickly through a cañon pass.
Over the mountains we went swiftly,
trying to find our horses grass.
Past the station we boldly went,
now along the riverside,
And our horses being spent,
of course we had to hide.

In the night we would travel,
in the daytime try and rest,
And throw ourselves on gravel,
to sleep we would try our best.
Around us our horses were stamping,
looking for hay or grain.
On the road the posse was tramping,
looking for us in vain.
One more day they would not have got us,
but my horse got sore and thin,

> And my partner was a mean cuss,
> so Billy Truman roped us in.
> Thirty years my partner got, I was given five.
> He seemed contented with his lot,
> and I am still alive.

Ed Simmons got hold of that one and passed it around the yard. For a day or two I was famous, and he told me that Joe Boot laughed out loud when he saw it. Looking at it later, I laughed even harder. Clearly I wasn't a writer, and certainly no poet.

My memoirs, as I called them, turned out to be nothing but a list of regrets that depressed me to the point of ripping the pages into shreds and tossing them into the yard. Simmons made me pick up every piece, saying: "There's enough trash as it is in this place," and he bird-dogged me as I moved around with a bucket, always there, always so close that, when I stood up, I brushed against him. He was trouble waiting to happen. I knew it, but I was powerless to change the situation.

Then they brought in another prisoner, a little brown woman whose eyes seemed to hold all the anguish of the world.

"Company, Pearl."

Ed unlocked the cell and shoved the woman inside. It was a cruel act, and unnecessary. A good wind would have blown her away.

"Quit pushing her," I said.

He frowned. "Shut up. She don't deserve better."

Then he slammed the door and locked it.

"Hey!" I called after him. "It's time to let me out!"

"Not till she settles down, it isn't."

She didn't seem to need settling. About my height, she was so thin she reminded me of one of those fallen, veined leaves you can almost see through. She wore her hair in a single, long braid that was black and so heavy it tilted her head back, making her seem always to be looking up to the ceiling, or to heaven.

"My name's Pearl Hart," I said.

She didn't answer, just lay down on her cot, and curled into a ball like she was defending herself. I understood that posture. I'd done it myself too many times to count.

"I'm not going to hurt you," I said gently.

Still she was silent, and I wondered if she was mute or if they'd shut me up with a mad woman.

Cautiously I sat down on the edge of her cot. "Hey," I said, "we're in here together, and I'm glad of it, but you have to tell me your name. I'm tired of talking to myself."

She opened her eyes, and I saw the pain in them. And then she spoke. "My name's Tally." It was a whisper, like a breeze had passed through, or a bird.

"So you *can* talk."

She nodded and closed her eyes.

"Well good," I said. "Take a nap if that's what you want. I'll be right here. Obviously I'm not going anywhere."

I laughed, but when I got no response and bent over her, I saw she had fallen asleep.

For the first few days all Tally did was sleep. At meal times she picked at her food and left most of it. Thin as she was, she seemed to be disappearing while I watched. Whatever crime she'd committed was destroying her from the inside, but prison etiquette, like the etiquette of the frontier, kept me from asking.

Finally, one evening as she turned away from the table and sat staring blindly out, I came to a decision. Whatever she'd done wasn't worth suicide.

"Look," I said, moving to sit beside her, "you've got to eat. No sense starving yourself, and the food's not that bad."

She sighed, one of those little sounds she made that were hardly sounds at all. "Leave me be," she said.

"That's what I'm not going to do," I told her. "I've been sitting here, watching you turn into a ghost, and I don't like it."

"Then don't watch."

"I'm stuck in here with you. But I'll be damned if I'll be stuck in here with a corpse."

One corner of her mouth twitched, and it almost seemed she was smiling. Then she said: "That'd be something, wouldn't it?"

I went along. "About as much fun as you've been all week."

"Why do you care?" She looked at me for the first time. "You don't know me or what I done."

Why, indeed? Maybe because she reminded me of my old self — hurting and no one to tell.

"Everybody needs a friend," I said. "Since we're in here together, we can at least be that."

"Don't want no friends," she muttered, turning away.

Oh, she was irritating! I could feel my temper rising. "That's what you think. There've been times I'd have killed for a friend. Just to be able to talk, to let out what's inside." I stood up and looked down at her. "If you ask me, what's inside you is killing you. I don't give a damn why you're in here. I just feel sorry that you hurt, because I know how it feels to hurt. Now I've said all I'm going to. What you do is up to you."

I went back to my dinner. It had grown cold, and fat floated on top of the stew. Hardly appetizing, but I ate it anyhow, and watched her while I chewed.

She was wrestling with herself, that was plain. And she was weeping. I could see her bony shoulders shaking under the calico prison blouse. But she never made a sound, and it was eerie to see that little body dark against the red afterglow of

151

sunset, head bent in despair.

But I didn't move or speak. There comes a time when you have to save yourself on your own, take charge of living or dying. I'd learned that much in my solitary days as I looked back at my own history. I knew where I'd gone wrong and why, but it was too late to change the past. The present and the future, though, were still mine.

So I sat, and the sky faded to purple, and the bats came out, swooping across the yard like tiny black kites. I'd always been afraid of bats until I got to Yuma and watched them, so small, so quick, so determined to live. I heard the rustle of her skirt and saw her turn halfway toward me, and still I waited, saying nothing.

Then, in a voice so small I could hardly make out her words, she said: "I killed my baby. I killed my child. I rocked her in my arms and sang, and put her in the canal. I watched her little face go under. Then I ran."

Silence. Bat wings fluttering. A boat whistle screaming like a lost soul, and the scent of citrus flowers like a drug in the night air.

"Why?" I was afraid to say any more.

She stood up, eyes blazing, anger and pain giving her strength. "Why? You ask me why, white woman? I'll tell you why. 'Cause I didn't want a life like I had for my child. 'Cause I had no food, no milk, no place to go, and she was hungry and crying. 'Cause I was nobody. I was black. 'Cause I didn't even know who her daddy was, and no home. I should've killed myself, too. Sunk down in that black water, holding her in my arms, and gone to Jesus with her. But I didn't, and that's my shame and my crime. I killed the only thing ever made a difference."

The fire went out of her suddenly, and she sat down again. Then she said: "You still want to be my friend, white woman?

You woman enough for that?"

In all my life I've never refused a dare. I got up and sat down close beside her and, looking straight into her face, said: "Tally, I'm woman enough for anything."

Her smile surprised me. It smoothed out her face, turned her young in spite of the tears, until she looked no more than a child herself.

"I bet you are at that," was all she said.

Chapter Thirty

Inevitably, my mother wrote to me — a long, disapproving letter that read in part:

Imagine how I felt, sitting in that hospital and finding that my daughter was a criminal talked about in all the papers, by all the nurses, all my friends? What went through your head? What <u>possessed</u> you?

And what of your children? You can hardly expect them not to find out about their mother. You have placed an unnecessary burden on innocent shoulders by your thoughtless, impulsive actions.

I sighed, and Tally, who had been watching me, asked: "Bad news?"

"A letter from my mother."

"She scolding you?"

I nodded.

"A little late for that," she said, "but mamas have to scold. That's what they do best."

"I never scolded my children," I said, remembering how we had bonded together in love, and for protection. "Did your mother scold you?"

Tally shrugged. "Honey, my mama was too busy to notice what I got into."

Her mother had been a laundress for the buffalo soldiers, moving with them from camp to camp, fort to fort all over the Southwest, and dragging her daughter along.

That much Tally had told me. But getting information out of her was like squeezing water out of a cactus. I never knew when I'd be pricked by a thorn.

"I was watched over till I thought I'd scream," I said. "It's better your way."

"Don't look like they did too good a job on either one of us," she said, "but at least you got your children." Her voice broke. In those early days she was never far from tears.

Sometimes I felt like *she* was my child, like I was her mother, and had to comfort her. It was a new experience for me — to care for someone, an adult, a woman who was as different from me as I was from my mother, yet in many ways similar. We were both grieving — for our children and for our lost innocence.

I continued skimming the letter and went on to the second page where a name leaped out at me.

"Frank's dead!" I exclaimed, shocked.

"Good riddance."

"She says nobody knows what happened to him. But his things were sent back to Toledo."

"How you feel about it?" Tally asked. "Like a widow?"

I put down the letter, walked to the door, and looked out. How *did* I feel, now that I was free of him forever? Perhaps a little sad, as if a part of my youth was gone. "Beautiful dreamer, wake unto me. . . ." So many promises, and so little to show for them. In spite of everything, I felt sorrow for that girl who believed in story books.

"I feel kind of sad," I said. "It's hard to explain. I hated him at the end, but there were good days. And my babies."

She put her arms around me. "You want to cry, go on," she said.

But the moment of sympathy exploded around us when Ed Simmons arrived with another prisoner who took one look into

155

our cell and began screaming in a mixture of Spanish and English.

"You think to put me in a cage with these *tortillieras!* Me, Rosa Alvarado. I won't do it! Let me go!" She struggled in his grasp, a tall woman, and strong. He had all he could do to push her inside and slam the door.

"Calm down, Rosa, or you'll go in the hole," he said.

She pounded on the bars. "Better there with the snakes than here!" she shouted. Then she went to the back of the cell, as far away from us as possible.

"Touch me," she snarled, "and I'll cut out your hearts!"

"Touch you?" I said, walking toward her. "Touch you! I wouldn't touch you with a stick. What's the matter with you, anyhow?"

She glared at me. "I know what you do," she said. "And it's a sin before God."

I called over my shoulder to Ed. "Get her out of here! She's crazy. *Loco,*" I added, for Rosa's benefit.

"Super's orders." He laughed. "Have a good time, ladies."

I watched him saunter across the yard, pleased with himself, and spat at his heels. Then I turned back to Rosa whose hair had come loose, and who was watching me through a tangle of dark red curls.

Somebody had to take charge, I thought, and it wasn't going to be Tally. She was sitting with her back to the wall, as far away from the newcomer as possible.

"My name's Pearl," I said. "And that's Tally. And everything was fine in here until you came. There's two of us, and one of you, and we don't like threats or shouting matches, so suppose you tell us what's bothering you."

"*Tortilliera!*" she spat out again. "Keep away!"

"I don't speak Spanish," I told her slowly, emphasizing

every word, "but I don't like being called names, so you'd better explain."

She had huge, dark eyes, nearly black, and they appraised me like I had fangs and horns.

"Look at you," she said finally, bitterly. "Pretending to be a man. *Pantalones*. Hair like a dog's ass, and a woman of your own. *¡Dios!* That I should end up in a cell with such people!"

Her accusation was so wild, it took me a minute to understand. Then I started to laugh and couldn't stop, even though it made her even angrier.

She stood up, a head taller than I was. "Don't you laugh at me!" she hissed. "Don't dare!"

"Now that's just enough!" Tally came out of her daze and pushed between us, a fierce terrier, holding off two mastiffs. She cocked her head and stared up at Rosa, and there was a toughness in her that I hadn't seen before, a kind of loyalty and courage that roused my admiration.

"You . . . ," she began. "You big, bad-mannered bitch. You come in here, not knowing nothing, throwing your weight around, disturbing the peace, and calling names. Who gave you the right? Who you think you are? You in jail, same as us, and you better figure how you gonna get along. We don't need you, but, sure as Satan, you need us." Then she snapped her mouth tightly shut and went back to her corner.

"Why, Tally!" I said, shocked.

She glared at Rosa. "Big, dumb bitch," she muttered. "There's no fault in women carin' for each other. Who else we got?"

"She's right," I said to Rosa. "And you're all wrong. I wear pants because I like them. I'm as much woman as you are."

"Don't you be comparing yourself with her," Tally said. "She ain't fit to clean your shoes."

Rosa said: "You don't know how you look. How I feel. Me,

157

Rosa Alvarado in jail with two lovers!"

Oddly, she laughed, her anger gone as quickly as it had come. "I have had enough of love. Of any kind. You understand me?"

"How come all's women talk about is love?" Tally wanted to know. "Ain't there anything else?"

Rosa's teeth flashed white. "It's what we know best," she said. "Love. And hate."

I said: "I thought I loved my husband. I guess I did for a while. And then I hated him."

"Did you kill him?" She looked interested for the first time. "I ran away."

"Cowards run. Me, I try to kill my Julio when he beat me for taking a lover. I tell him, for beating me, I will cut off his *cojones* while he watch." She made a slicing gesture, and I shivered.

"Did you?"

She shook her head. "His brothers, they catch me, and send me here. But not before I made many marks. Like the ones he made on me."

The ugliness of it all took hold of me. The waste. The pain. Three women jailed, two of them for murder or its attempt. And why? Because nothing was fair, and life at its best was hard. Because simple dignity was something worth fighting for, even knowing it was a losing battle.

I looked out into the yard. A bitter wind was blowing, and the sky was pale and cold. Winter had come. In the spring we would still be here, three women condemned because of ignorance — our own and the world's.

"Welcome to hell," I said to Rosa.

She tossed her heavy hair. "I been in hell," she said. "Without Julio, I am in paradise."

Tally chuckled, a dry sound like stones rattling. "She may be right at that," she said. "She just might be right."

158

Chapter Thirty-One

In the spring, Joe Boot escaped, and the prison superintendent sent for me.

"Why does he want me? I don't know anything," I said to Ed Simmons, as he walked me to the office. "I haven't even seen Joe since I've been here."

"Don't tell me. Tell him," he said. "And don't get me in any trouble, or you'll be sorry."

I stopped walking. "How could I do that?"

"By running off at the mouth like all women."

"Did anybody ever tell you that you're a son-of-a-bitch?" I asked.

His hand was heavy on my arm, and he pressed tighter. "You watch your mouth, Pearl, and mind your manners. Or else."

I was bored. Restless. Looking for a fight that would light up the dullness. "Or else what?" I challenged.

"Or else you'll be sorry." He ran his tongue across his lips that were the color of raw liver. "Then again, maybe you won't."

He was repulsive . . . a toad . . . one of those poisonous, bloated creatures that hop along the banks of the river and take nourishment from crawling insects and the thickness of mud.

I said: "Don't threaten me."

He smiled. "It's not a threat. It's a promise." And the look on his face filled me with horror, so much so that when I finally stood in front of Herbert Brown, the super, I was speechless.

159

Brown was a kindly man, but stern. "Sit down, Pearl," he ordered. And to Simmons: "Wait outside."

I relaxed when the door shut and Brown and I were alone, facing each other.

Before he had a chance to question me, I said: "I haven't seen Joe since I was brought here. I don't know anything."

"But you might know about his family."

I shook my head. "He never mentioned his family, and that's the truth."

"Where was he from?"

"I don't know that, either. He said, a long time ago, he'd been on his own since he was a kid, and I believed him."

He frowned, and two little lines marked the space between his eyebrows. "So you can't tell me where he might be headed."

"No, sir." I squirmed in my chair.

"Sit still!" he commanded suddenly. "What are you afraid of?"

"Nothing." Simmons probably had his ear glued to the door.

"Are they treating you all right?" came the next question.

"Yes." I figured the shorter I kept my answers, the better it would be for me.

Brown sighed. "All right. You can go. But if you remember anything that might help, you'll tell me." It was another order.

I nodded.

In my mind, I pictured Joe in Mexico, but that was imagination. He could just as easily have stowed away on one of the river steamers and gone north to the mines where the desert stretched its lean body for miles, or all the way to Port Isabel and from there out to sea. I wished for a moment that I'd escaped, too, that we were both running again with the land in front of us, or the ocean, this time smarter than before.

I was brought back to reality by the sight of a stocky figure crossing the yard toward us. It couldn't be! I squinted in the glare and then pulled free of Simmons.

"Dan!" I called, running as fast as I could. "Here I am!"

He spread his arms wide and stopped my flight. "Ah, Pearl, you damned fool," he said in greeting, "what've you got yourself into?"

I didn't answer. I was too happy to see Dan Sandeman, one of the few who had ever treated me kindly, been concerned for me without asking for payment.

"Why are you here?" I asked him. "How'd you get here?"

He stepped back and eyed me, shaking his head. "I came to see you, and what do I find? A ragamuffin. What happened to the Pearl I knew?"

"It's a long story."

"I've got all afternoon."

Simmons caught up with us. "Who are you?" he demanded. But he couldn't shake Dan.

"An old friend. There's no rule against visiting prisoners, I assume."

"Nope. But I'll have to lock you in her cell. Her buddy just broke out, and I can't take chances with her following him."

I wanted to kill him. To grab his throat and squeeze him until his eyes popped, his face turned purple. I wanted, like Rosa, to cut off his *cojones* and throw them at him. But I held my tongue, even when Ed frisked Dan for hidden weapons, turning up only cigarettes, a bottle of cologne, and a bag of oranges.

"Gotta be careful," he explained.

Dan kept his face expressionless. "Certainly."

"He's just throwing his weight around," I muttered. "Don't pay any attention to him."

Dan followed me into the cell where Tally and Rosa looked up, astonished. To me he whispered: "Just take it easy, for God's sake. What's got into you?"

161

"Everything!" I turned on him. "This place. Simmons out there with his filthy mind. Nothing to do but sit here and read old newspapers. You wouldn't like it, either."

"Whose fault is it?" he wanted to know, quirking an eyebrow. "And who are these ladies?"

"We're not ladies. We're bodies with numbers."

"Christ, how you've changed," was his reply. Then he bowed to Rosa who had come up to us, rustling her skirts.

"It's a pleasure to see a real gentleman," she said, smiling. "Here we see only thieves and murderers and the pigs who guard them."

She was flirting with him openly and seductively, and suddenly I was furious. I grabbed his arm and steered him away.

"This is Tally," I said.

She made a noise that might have been a hello and went back to her lace making. From dawn to dark she worked at it, turning out lace as delicate as spider webs — collars, cuffs, runners, trim by the yard — and sold it, too, in the prison store. "It helps," she had explained. "You ought to try."

But I lacked the patience and the talent and, as a result, found myself back writing poems that Rosa made into songs. From somewhere she'd gotten an old guitar she treated as if it were priceless, polishing it and gently tightening the strings. And it was the guitar that Dan noticed, lying on the table, its curved sides shining in a ray of sun.

"Who plays?" he wanted to know.

"Rosa. I write the words and sing. We're good, too. When we get out, we're going on the road."

"You mean *if* you get out," Tally corrected.

"I could use you two," Dan said. "I've been on my own since I left Chicago. Play something."

Rosa didn't wait to be asked twice. She picked up the guitar, caressing it with long fingers, bending gracefully over it as she

162

tuned. When she was satisfied, she looked up and flashed Dan a smile.

"First, the songs of my country," she announced and played the mournful opening bars of an old Mexican song that she had, over many weeks, taught me to sing in Spanish.

I sang my heart out for nearly an hour, and, when we'd finished, Dan applauded long and hard.

"You two are dynamite. How long before you're out?"

Rosa shrugged. "Who can say? Me, they give six years."

"Too long," I said. "Too damned long."

Dan's eyes were bright. He was thinking ahead. I hadn't spent all those months with him without learning how his mind worked.

"Look," he said finally, "when you're out, get in touch with me. Oh, I'll be on the road somewhere . . . they don't call me 'The Wandering Jew' for no reason. But I'll keep in touch. There's money, playing these towns, and it's fun. You meet people, learn things, see the country. How about it, ladies?"

Rose brought her fingers down in a loud chord. "I, for one, say yes," she said. "We'll find you, *Señor* Dan. And we will sing and play our poor hearts out when you tell us."

Dan bowed low. "At your service, *señora*," he promised.

I didn't respond, but Tally, as usual, had the last word.

"It sound like horse shit to me," she said.

Chapter Thirty-Two

When Dan had gone, Tally spoke up again. We were sopping up our bowls of beans and bacon with our bread when she started.

"Must be the sight of a man makes you both hungry."

Rosa and I stopped eating, our dripping bread halfway to our mouths. Tally grinned at the sight, one of those painful facial gestures she was so good at.

"Yeah," she said. "You might as well stop feeding yourselves and listen."

"Listen to what?" I asked.

"To me," she said. "I got eyes. And ears, too. And a brain. And I see you both dreamin' about freedom and a man to go with it. When you gonna figure out you don't need no man? That you can do it on your own? Seems to me, it's men who got us all in trouble."

Rosa popped bread into her mouth. "Be quiet, little one," she warned. "I like you better when you don't talk."

Tally put down her spoon. "I don't care if you like me or not, but you gonna listen. And you ain't gonna like what you hear."

Curious, I leaned my elbows on the table. "Go ahead," I said.

She shot me a look. "Listen good, then. I'll start at the beginning . . . with my mama and the daddy I never knew. I'm a bastard, just like my own child was. Only it didn't mean much to me. I had my mama, and the soldiers, and they was nice to us both. We had enough to eat, and a roof over us, most times, and that's all I ever wanted. I didn't have no dreams, see, 'cause I didn't know there was anything to dream about."

"*Ai,*" Rosa murmured. "*Pobrecita.*"

Tally smiled. "Yeah. *Pobrecita.* Only I was too dumb to know it. Things went on. The Army moved, and we moved with it, walkin' and ridin' in old wagons all the way from Texas across that desert to Arizona. And then one day my mama died. Passed out in her wash tub and never woke up. After that I was on my own. Oh, they was nice to me. I was a kid, and homeless, and the colonel's wife took me in to nurse her babies." Her face softened at the memory. "They was nice babies, and I loved them. I rocked them in my arms and sang them songs, and never thought about the future . . . theirs or mine."

She pushed back from the table and started to walk, back and forth, back and forth, her heels thudding on the ground like drumbeats.

"Then the colonel got transferred, and the new man didn't have kids, so I was out of a job. It was the first time in my life I realized death was just around the corner, and it was up to me to keep him away."

Knowing how she must have felt, I nodded in agreement.

"The colonel's wife gave me a letter. It said how good I was with children, and she sent me to town to a lady she knew. And the first thing that lady said when she see me was . . . 'I never hire colored help.' It took me a minute to figure she meant me. Me! Nobody ever called me that before, and it hurt, but I said . . . 'Try me for a week.' And she did, and, when the week was up, she said . . . 'All right, Tally, you can stay. As long as you behave yourself.' She had cold eyes, just like a snake's. I didn't mind the babies, just her, always waitin' for me to make a mistake. I had all the chores, too. It was like I didn't have feelings or a body that got so tired I couldn't hardly move around. But I stayed. I didn't have no choice." She stopped then, blinking away tears.

I said: "It's all right. You don't have to tell us."

She turned on me, fierce as a wounded animal. "Yes I do," she hissed. "You been sayin' how what's inside is killin' me, and that's the truth. So I'm lettin' it out, and you gonna sit there and hear it. Every word. Like it or not."

She went back to pacing. "I had every other Sunday off, and I used to go out in the fields and smell that sweet air, and stick my feet in the water just like a little kid. Sometimes, I'd take me a nap, and, when I woke up, I'd feel like the Lord had just created the world and me in it, and I'd be happy for the littlest time out there with the sky and the water and the plants growing.

"But one day I woke up and . . ." — her voice trembled — "and they was four men sittin' there, watching me. I knew they were trouble and tried to run, but they brought me down, and then they had their way with me. Each and every one. Hard and quick, like they'd do to a whore, and laughing and grunting like the hogs they were."

She shuddered. "I can still see their ugly faces. And smell 'em, too. Sweat, dirt, stinking lust. When they finished, they left me lyin' there. Just went off and left me. Maybe they thought I was dead. I don't know. But I was scared to move for fear they'd come back and start again, maybe kill me. They didn't, and I got up and washed off in the ditch, and drug myself back to town. I never said nothin'. What was there to say? Who could I tell? Nobody'd believe me. Not that woman with the glass eyes. So I went on workin', and then found out a child was coming."

She whirled around, staring at us with the eyes of a madwoman. "You think I wanted that baby? You think I was gonna

166

love it? I tried every which way to get rid of it, but it stuck, fastened on me like a snail in my belly. I hated it. And I hated it worse when I got turned out of that house for being a loose woman, not fit to be around white babies. Then I had to steal my food or beg. I had to sleep wherever I could find a place. And that baby was born in a barn in a pile of hay, and no one to care for either one of us.

"And then, a funny thing. I looked at her, and I saw those big eyes, those little hands and feet so helpless but so sure of livin' . . . and I fell in love. I never been in love. And I won't ever be again. Love's a knife in your belly. It tears out your heart, so's all you are is skin walking around, and you emptied out. And I was empty. I didn't have no milk to feed her. I didn't have nothin'. I went to the sheriff, and he turned me out. That's right, turned me out like I wasn't even a person. And all the time that baby screamin' and hungry, and gettin' weaker. Both of us fit to die right on the street, and nobody to help. *Nobody!*"

She screamed out the word, and I was scared. She seemed like she was in a trance, back on the street, and living the horror all over again. I wanted to stop her, but Rosa put a hand on my arm.

"Let her finish," she whispered.

And so we sat there, side by side in silence, while Tally fought through her nightmare a second time.

"Seems like then I lost my mind," she went on. "I went out of my head. I went back to those fields where it all started, with that baby in my arms, still cryin', but softer, like she didn't have no more strength. And I looked down and saw the life goin' out of her, like a door closing, inch by inch, and I vowed I'd make it easy. Why should dyin' be so hard? Why should a child have to suffer, and maybe live to suffer more? So I put her in the water, gentle as I could, and watched her sink. Her face like a little flower, her arms reachin' out to me like she was sayin' . . . 'Save me!' But I had saved her. And that water was like a baptism. She never done no harm, that child. 'Twas me that done it, bringing her into this world that had no use for her or me.

"And now I'm here, payin' all over again, and what they don't none of them know is that I'll be payin' ever' day I spend on this earth. Seein' it happen, when I close my eyes and when I open them. That baby I loved, and the water takin' her in. And those men that did it . . . those men went free. They out there, doin' to every woman what they done to me. You think that's fair? If you do, you better start thinkin' some more."

Then she lay down on her cot and curled up as she had done on her first day, as if she were protecting herself from all harm and all memory.

Chapter Thirty-Three

Tally was still sleeping the next morning, so small, so still on her cot that I thought she was dead.

Rosa put her fingers to her lips. "It's good that she sleep," she whispered. "Leave her."

In the pale light of early morning, Rosa looked like a statue, tall, with broad shoulders, and a smile that reminded me of a painting I'd seen in a church. I wondered at the change in her. No longer the screaming shrew, she was, instead, someone I trusted, even leaned on. There was strength in her, and compassion, and a natural wisdom that seemed to have its roots in the earth.

"How do you know so much?" I asked, also whispering.

She looked from Tally to me with those bottomless, dark eyes, and it seemed as if she, too, was remembering the cruelties of her past, had carried them with her into our cell.

"My *abuela* is a *curandera*," she said, keeping her voice low. "When I was little, I went with her to the mountains, to the little fields along the rivers to find the herbs, and sometimes I watched while she helped the sick and called out their devils. I learned many things. Many times she tell me that sleep is better than medicines, that our bodies know more than any doctor. You understand this?"

"I guess," I said, not sure what she meant or whether to believe in her grandmother's home remedies.

Rosa glanced over at Tally. "Yesterday," she said, "she let out the devil in her. Now sleep cures the marks of his claws."

In a strange way, what she was saying made sense, the same

way religion made sense, at least to me. Some things you couldn't see, but took on faith. I had always been skeptical.

"If she isn't awake by this afternoon, I'm calling the doctor," I said.

Rosa scowled. She hated opposition. "He will tell you the same thing."

"Asking him won't hurt, will it?"

"It's a waste of time. Besides, you are asking for yourself, not for her."

I laughed. She had a way of slicing straight to the truth, uncomfortable sometimes, but comforting, too. I always knew where I stood in her opinion — not a bad thing, in prison or out.

"I think you like this doctor," she said. "Better even than your *Señor* Dan."

"You wish I did!" I retorted, seeing where she was headed.

"*Señor* Dan is a good man," she purred. "If you had stayed with him, you wouldn't be in here."

It was, again, the truth. I'd have been on the road, singing with a man who genuinely cared about me. Maybe we'd even have been in a house of our own. There would have been no children, at least not the ones I had. At the thought of Emma and Joe, I stopped dreaming.

"Well, I didn't," I said. "He asked me, but I was too scared to go with him. Frank had me so I couldn't think from one minute to the next. He had me believing I was dumb and helpless, and without him to take care of me I'd probably die. Then he'd beat me to make sure I knew just how helpless I was. That's how I lived. It's different now. At least, I hope so."

"For you, I hope so, too," she said. "And for me. Maybe little Tally was right. Maybe we do not need men like we think."

"We don't need Frank or your Julio, anyhow. We're better off in here, which sounds funny. At least, we're thinking for ourselves."

"As long as we don't lie to ourselves," she said. "Seeing the truth is hard."

"Not with you around, it isn't."

She was pleased. I could see it in the way she tried not to smile and failed. "It's better so," she answered finally. "You take your life and do what you know to be right, and never mind what they tell you . . . the old ones, the cowards, the husbands forced on you, the priests who believe you must suffer." She spat on the floor as if she had tasted bitter herbs. "Suffering," she went on in a hard voice, "is for fools. I know this. Here, and here." She pointed to her head, then to her breast. "We three have suffered enough."

I said: "I've been a fool most of my life."

"But no more." Her eyes burned like candles, and something in them suggested prayer and healing, and for the first time in years I felt at ease, at peace, as if I belonged in a body that was completely my own.

Happily, I couldn't see the future, couldn't know that I, my body, and my self would not be mine much longer.

That afternoon I sent for Milton Tatum. Tally was still deeply asleep, and I was worried.

The doctor came immediately, good man that he was, and he asked us questions, some of which we didn't know how to answer.

"How long has she been like this?"

"Almost twenty-four hours," I said.

"Why? What happened?"

Rosa and I looked at each other and spread our hands in a gesture of helplessness. Then Rosa said: "She let out the devil. Now she is at peace."

"Don't let her die!" I pleaded. "Help her, please!"

"Right now the biggest danger is dehydration," he said. "We have to get liquid in her, however we can." He lifted her into a sitting position and gestured for me to bring water.

Together we spooned it into her mouth and watched as she swallowed. He made sure she was breathing easily, then put her back down on her cot, and turned to me.

"Give her water, just like we did now. Every hour, as much as she'll take. And call for me if there's a problem, or if she seems feverish."

"Tally can't die!"

He took my hands in his. They were warm hands, strong, and I responded to the feel of them.

"She's undernourished," he explained. "And bearing a burden of guilt we can't begin to understand. It's up to you two to bring her back. And up to her if she wants to die." His eyes were kind and steady.

Rosa came to stand with him. "She will live," she pronounced, her voice deep as an organ. "I tell you this because it is so."

The doctor bowed his head. "I'll come first thing in the morning," he said. And as he left, he pressed my hands.

Rosa didn't miss the gesture. "So!" she said. "It isn't only you."

I wasn't in any mood to discuss my feelings. "I'll take first watch," I said, remembering Joe and vowing to stay awake, regardless. Tally's death wasn't going to be on my head.

"Call me when you want," Rosa said. "Me, I don't need so much sleep."

Together we spent the night watching, praying, because Tally's fight had become our own, and, if she died, then something in us would die without ever having the chance to flower.

172

We didn't talk about it. I'm not sure we even knew what we were feeling during those long, dark hours. Knowledge came later — many years later, in my case. All I knew for certain that night was, if Tally went, something in me would go with her, some belief, some raw courage, some dream I hadn't dreamed yet, but that lay in the years ahead.

And so we took turns, Rosa and me, spooning water into her mouth, putting damp rags on her forehead, and watching her thin, brown face for signs of life or struggle.

What I remember most about that night is the voice of the wind, the sand blowing through the iron bars, and how the river, on the rise, rumbled at the base of the prison walls with a sound like distant thunder.

In the morning, Tally opened her eyes.

"I been asleep," she said.

Our relief was so great that we burst out laughing, while Tally looked at us in amazement.

"Did I miss something?" she wanted to know.

"Not a thing," I answered.

"Then why you two acting so funny?"

Rosa took charge. "Because you slept for two nights and a day, my friend. Because we thought you would die."

"I might die from hunger if that monkey don't bring breakfast," came Tally's answer.

I went to the door and yelled for Ed, who came grumbling. "What's all the racket?"

"Get Doctor Tatum. And breakfast. His patient's hungry."

"Pretty quick with orders, ain't you?"

Why was it, I wondered, that he was so detestable? Maybe it took his type to work in a prison, or maybe he simply enjoyed being a bully.

I stamped my foot. "Just do it. Call the doctor. Or open

up, and I'll go get him."

"All right, all right. Keep your shirt on."

He walked slowly across the yard, and I vowed revenge on him. *Some day,* I said to myself. *Some day, I'll be out of here, and I'll find you. Just wait.*

"Why you callin' the doc? I ain't sick," Tally said.

"Because it gives her pleasure to see him," Rosa answered. "Be quiet, little one."

"Looks like all kinds of things been goin' on that I missed."

"You had us worried," I said.

She thought about that for a minute, looking down at her hands that were folded in her lap. "Nobody ever worried about me," she said finally. "Not even my mama."

"Well, it's past time somebody did," I said. "Way past."

She chuckled. "We make an odd bunch, don't we? Bad women and all sizes and colors."

"Color is for enemies," Rosa said. "Friends see only hearts."

Once again I marveled at how she could come to the point. "Where were you when *I* needed you?" I asked her.

She made a sweeping gesture with her hands. "I'm here now," she said.

Chapter Thirty-Four

I needed her desperately the day Ed Simmons and another guard, whose face I never clearly saw and whose name I never learned, dragged me into an empty cell and raped me. Ed took me by surprise as I was coming back from the prison dentist, miserable from having a painful tooth pulled. My mouth tasted like blood. I was biting down hard on a piece of cotton when he took my arm.

"Need help?" he asked.

"No. Can't talk," I mumbled through clenched teeth.

"That's a relief."

I glared at him — always there, always finding ways to insult or touch me. I detested his face, his close-set, pale eyes, and the way he always looked unclean, as if he needed a bath and a good shave. I tried to jerk loose, but, light-headed, I stumbled and fell against him. He took full advantage, putting his arms around me, pulling me close, so close I could smell his stinking breath.

"Let go!" I mumbled, afraid suddenly, realizing how small I was, how helpless.

"Not yet, sweetheart."

I watched his face change as he ran his hands down my body, and I twisted in his arms, trying to run. He only laughed deep in his throat like an animal.

"Not this time." He picked me up and started walking, not to my cell but to one on the end that was empty and that looked to me like the entrance to hell.

I writhed in his grip, and spat out the cotton, and with it

175

a clot of blood that landed on his cheek.

"Bitch," he said, and, as I started to scream, he clamped a hand over my mouth, calling to another guard over his shoulder.

"Gimme a hand here. I got a live one."

Oh, he gave a hand, all right, whoever he was, taking me so hard the blood ran down my throat and nearly choked me, after Simmons had rammed his way inside, not even stopping to take off his pants.

I lay there, remembering Frank and how, when he was in a rage, he would come at me, hard and quick as if I wasn't even human, thinking of a tree being chopped down in a forest, the axe biting deep, wounding to the core. I thought about dying, but death wouldn't come. What came was pain, anguish, and hatred. Wave after wave of it — hate, hate, hate. I wanted to kill them both. I wanted to destroy the world.

"You talk, and I'll deny it," Simmons hissed in my ear. "I'll say you been a trouble-maker from the start, and I'll put you in the snake pit till you die down there. You and your girl friends with you. You hear?"

I heard, but I lay with my eyes closed and didn't, couldn't, answer. Anything I said at that point would have brought me more pain.

The other guard said: "She's passed out on us." He sounded worried.

"No-good bitch." Ed was buttoning his fly. "She'll be all right. Tough as nails, this one. Needed a lesson. Needed a good fuck."

My whole body trembled as I lay there, listening. "A good fuck!" What I needed, what I had always needed, was kindness. Tenderness. Given those, I would have been able to give in return. Where was the man with gentle fingers, loving eyes, the ability to share? Where was Cal whose kindness was only

176

a memory? I was lost, a wanderer in the desert that was my home, a woman looking for comfort that glimmered like a mirage, tantalizing and always false.

Tears ran down my face and mixed with the blood in my mouth. I heard them leave, the two men, but I lay there a long time, too miserable to move, too bruised — heart and soul and body — to care.

When I finally got up and staggered down the row, Rosa met me. *"Madre de Dios,"* she said, and her voice seemed to echo off the stone walls and into the night. *"Madre de Dios,* what has happened?"

I couldn't tell her. Not then. I found my way to my cot and lay there in silence all through the dark night, alone as I had never been alone, and, outside, the hot wind, the flight of bats, the smell of the river pushing its way between its banks as those men had pushed their way into me — without thought, without feeling.

Alone in the dark, I cried until I hadn't any more tears, and then, blessedly, like Tally, I slept.

Chapter Thirty-Five

"You don't understand!"

In my mind I kept seeing Simmons's maddened face, kept reliving the shock, the horror of violation. Over and over, I saw it, felt it, as if the first time hadn't been enough. And further back there was Frank, his face twisted with rage and lust, and Burke in the alley in Phoenix, all of them after, not me, but that entrance to my body that gave them such pleasure and me only pain.

"No matter what," I said to Rose and Tally, "he'll say it was my fault. He can do it, don't you see? He hates me, and he'll take it out on all of us, put us in the pit till we go insane or die. We're prisoners. We don't have any rights."

Tally bristled. "Rights? Rights? Seems I heard that word before."

"Be quiet!" Rosa snapped. "We must think what to do."

"Nothing. We're not going to do anything." I pounded my fists on my knees. "If I ask to talk to the super, Simmons'll go with me, and he'll get me before I cross the yard. Then he'll come back for you. All I want is to be left alone. To not talk about it and try to forget. And never to see his face again. Never, never, never!"

I was screaming when he arrived with breakfast.

"Cut the racket!"

Rosa, wild-eyed, turned on him. "You little cockroach," she hissed. "Some day I will find you and I, myself, will pull off your little boy's parts with my hands and stick them in your mouth and make you eat them."

In her fury she seemed to tower over him, a dark angel set on revenge.

"Shut up, greaser." He shoved past her and plunked down our breakfast, and his tone, his arrogance, the still-vivid memory of what he'd done, turned me ice cold with anger.

Though I hadn't ever wanted to see him again, I got up and looked squarely in his face, and, when I started to talk, my voice didn't sound like my own. It came out hard and mean, the way I felt.

"I'm going to tell you something, and I want you to remember it. When I get out of here, I'm going to get you. I'm going to make you suffer like you made me suffer. You won't know when, and you won't know where, but I'll get you. So you better be watching your back trail because I'll be on it. And the worse you treat any of us now, the worse it'll be for you later. Now get out of here."

For a minute nobody moved or spoke, then Simmons grinned, uneasily, because I'd obviously shaken him. I took advantage of the silence to drive home my point.

"And if you ever . . . *ever* . . . call Rosa a greaser again, it'll go worse for you. Remember that."

He spun on his heel and left, quickly for once.

"*¡Dios!*" Rosa exclaimed.

"*Dios* my foot," I said. "I got mad. I got mad at the whole bunch . . . Frank, Julio, those men who hurt Tally. They all came together, all of a sudden, and he took the rap. I'd have killed him if I had a gun."

"But you *will* kill him?" Rosa looked hopeful.

"I'll do something."

"And I will help."

A month later I threw up my breakfast. When I'd thrown

179

up three days in a row, we sat around the table and looked at each other.

"You better go see your friend, the doctor," Rosa said at last.

"No. I'm all right."

"Honey," Tally said, "you ain't all right. Least it don't seem so. Better go get looked over."

So I went. And when he'd examined me, Milton Tatum shook his head.

"How?" he asked sadly. "How, Pearl?"

"I can't say." I sat up on the examining table. "I can't tell you, and I don't have to. But I want you to get rid of it."

He bent his head. "I'm sorry. I can't do that."

"Why not?"

"I took an oath."

"Bullshit!" I wriggled off onto the floor and pulled down my skirt. "I don't want this baby! You hear me? It was rape, and I'm telling you that much so you'll do something."

He took my hands and pulled me close. "Pearl," he said. "I can't. It's against what I believe. Do you understand?"

I didn't. He was an idealist, but I was carrying the child of a man I detested down to my bones. Without hesitating, I slapped his face. "You damned fool!" I yelled. "You hypocrite!"

He refused to look at me. "Yes," he said. "I am those things. But I value life."

"Life!" I snorted. "What you know about life you could fit in your ear."

Then I ran for the cell — home, haven, place of refuge where two others understood and shared my grief, my shame.

Chapter Thirty-Six

After days of thinking, I came up with a solution.

"We're getting out of here," I said. "All three of us. To-gether. At the same time."

"Hah!" Tally said. "You got fine dreams."

Rosa only watched me, halfway smiling. "Tell us."

I did. "I'm writing to the governor. And to the super. And I'm going to tell them I'm pregnant. That I got pregnant in their sacred jail. And if they don't pardon me . . . and the two of you . . . I'll make a national scandal. All those newspapers that loved my story will like this one even better. It's political, and it's true."

"How you mail these letters?" Rosa was doubtful.

"The doctor. He's my friend. At least, I hope he is. And when he's asked, he'll have to tell them the truth."

Rosa handed me paper and a pencil. "Then write. Write for all of us."

So I wrote. And Milton Tatum, as I knew he would, told the truth in letters of his own.

He said to me: "For God's sake, I'd marry you myself if I hadn't a wife already."

That made me laugh. "I wouldn't have you. No offense."

"Ah, Pearl."

"Ah, Pearl, nothing," I said. "You're a nice man, but I wouldn't have you."

He looked ashamed, and I was glad. Once I'd found him attractive. Now he was only another in a long list of men who didn't live up to what seemed to be their promises.

"Pearl. The super wants you." It was Simmons. Always there was Simmons and his evil face. I thought he would haunt my dreams for the rest of my life.

"What for?" I pretended innocence.

"He didn't say."

I took Rosa's hand, then Tally's. "We're all going."

"He don't want them. Just you."

Hand in hand, the three of us advanced toward him.

"Simmons," I said, "I'm not walking anywhere in this prison alone. For good reason. Got it?"

"Damn you." He looked worried.

"No. Damn *you*. Now let's go."

If Herbert Brown was surprised to see all of us, he didn't let it show. "Sit down, ladies," he said.

My letter lay on his desk, and he looked from it to me. "This is a serious matter, Pearl."

A smart retort rose to my lips, but I squelched it. "Yes," was all I said.

"Further, Doctor Tatum confirms the fact that you are, indeed . . . er . . . with child."

The whole situation was horrifying to him. His feelings showed plainly on his face, and also his fear that he might — in fact, would — lose his job if word got out.

I said nothing, just folded my hands and waited. Beside me, I could feel Rosa's tension mounting.

"Can you tell me how such a thing came about?"

I took a deep breath. "No, sir. I can't. At least not yet."

"Why not?"

"Because I can't."

"Are you afraid? Is someone threatening you? Tell me. Perhaps I can help."

How could I trust him? I weighed the aspects and

decided that I couldn't.

"When I'm free . . . when I'm outside these walls with a pardon, and these ladies with me, then I'll tell you," I said. "That's a promise."

"I see." But he didn't . . . couldn't see. He was a man, and he had never been at the mercy of another's strength or brutality, never had his person violated by another.

"I meant what I wrote," I told him. "I won't have a child born in a prison. The child is innocent, and I pray it remains so. I want to be released, and I want these women released with me. Otherwise, I'll tell the whole unhappy story to the papers." I leaned forward in my chair and put my hands flat on his desk. "And I will do it, Mister Brown. That's a promise, too."

He was silent a minute, probably seeing the newspaper headlines in his imagination.

BANDIT QUEEN GIVES BIRTH IN YUMA PRISON
ORGIES IN PRISON SAYS PEARL HART

Oh, they'd have fun with this story, and it would cost him his job. He knew it, and so did I.

He sighed. "This is blackmail, as you no doubt realize."

"Call it what you like," I said.

Again he sighed. He knew when he was beaten. "I'll have to speak to the governor," he said. "I don't have the authority to grant your pardon. Or pardons for these women."

I played my trump card. "I've already written to him."

Slowly he sat back in his chair. "My God, woman," he said.

Once again I curbed a smile. "I meant what I said, Mister Brown. I will not . . . absolutely will *not* . . . give birth to a child in this jail or any other. It's up to you. And, of course, the governor."

183

"It will take a while," he said. "These things aren't arranged overnight."

"Any time within the next two months will be fine," I assured him. "After that . . . well, my condition will be obvious, and I don't think you want that."

"I never wanted women here at all," he said. "They're nothing but trouble. As you have proved." He stood up. "You may go now. And I trust you'll behave yourselves."

His tone was insulting. "Mister Brown," I said, "I have behaved myself from the moment I entered this place. What happened was not my fault, but the fault of your administration."

Then I took Tally's and Rosa's hands and swept out the door with as much arrogance as I could muster.

Chapter Thirty-Seven

It was the longest month I've ever known, waiting for a pardon that might not come, for a summons to Brown's office, for a word of hope, any word at all, while trying to hide the fact that I was sick every morning as soon as I looked at breakfast. Tally and Rosa did their best to calm me down, as I alternated between tears and fits of anger.

"I hate being a woman! I hate having babies! I hate this baby! I wish I was dead!" Like a crazy person I paced the cell, slamming my fists into the stone walls and kicking the furniture.

"This baby's gonna get us out of here," Tally said. "And you don't hate it. You ain't even laid eyes on it yet."

"A lot you know!" The words burst out, and then I was sorry and said so, forgetting my own misery at the sight of her face.

"I'm the only one of us does know," she answered. "And I'm telling you, so's you'll feel better. You can't hate no baby, whatever else you feel."

"It's his, damn it! How am I going to love his brat? Every time I see it, I'll think of him."

She shook her head. "No you won't. And, besides, maybe it's the other fella's."

"That's supposed to make a difference?"

"No, honey. But I'm telling you, that a child is innocent and you got to do for it, come what may." She put her hands on her hips and faced me, and once again I thought of her as a fierce little terrier, fighting for her beliefs. "You helped me when I come in here and just wanted to die. Now it's my turn, and I'm telling you what you oughta know. You got other babies, and you hated their daddy, too. He beat you, and he raped you, but when they was born, you loved them, and you love them now. It'll be the same with this one. Wait and see."

"Besides," Rosa said, "we will all help. It will have three mamas. Lucky little *niño*."

In spite of myself, I recognized the truth of their logic. I had loved my children from the moment they were born, in spite of the circumstances of their conception and the pains of labor.

"Damn it, Tally, why can't you let me hate?"

"Hate a bad thing. It'll kill you sure as a bullet in your heart."

Rosa nodded. "It's true, what she says. Me, I don't hate Julio. I just hope never to see his face again. I hope he burns in hell!"

By this point we were all laughing, Rosa as much as Tally, and me at the contradictions in her speech.

"Crazy Mexican!" Tally teased.

"Poca negra," came the retort.

"What about me?" I asked.

Rosa threw up her hands. "You!" she exclaimed. "Who knows what to call you?"

We laughed harder. Some time, in the year we had spent together, we had forged a bond, and it was strong, and I knew it would carry us through the hardships of the next years of our lives without breaking.

At Rosa's urging, I wrote a note to Dan, telling him we were to be released.

"He will come for us," she prophesied.

"You hope," I said.

She only smiled.

Tally rolled her eyes. "That man's a rolling stone, and you

both past time to go traveling."

"And under the terms of these pardons, you will not return to Arizona until the time of your prison sentence has elapsed. Is that clear?"

Herbert Brown put down the letter from which he was quoting and waited for our response.

It came quickly. "Yes, sir."

"Good. You'll be released a week from today." He folded the letter, and it was obvious he was going to say something more. "I regret the circumstances," he went on, looking at me. "I hope you will not do anything foolish. The governor has made another condition for your pardon, and that is that you say nothing to anyone about what happened."

"What if I do?"

"Then you will be brought back to serve out your term."

Three more years! I swallowed hard. "I won't say anything. I promise."

"Good," he said again, and stood up. "I'll have street clothes for you and enough money to see you out of the territory. What are your plans?"

"We're going on the stage."

He looked surprised, then suspicious, as if I'd deceived him. "How is that possible?"

"It'll be possible for a few months," I said. "I have to earn some money somehow, and, under the circumstances, I can't very well go back home, much as I want to." I tried to keep the bitterness out of my voice, but failed.

"Ahh." To give him his due, he looked genuinely sorry. He put out his hand. "I regret this happened. More than you know."

"Not any more than I do, Mister Brown," I said, and the knowledge was like ashes in my mouth.

187

Chapter Thirty-Eight

"Hey, Pearl! How does it feel to be out?"

"What're your plans?"

"Where're you headed?"

The newspapermen were lined up outside the prison gates. It seemed there were a hundred of them, yapping like a pack of hounds, their faces greedy for a word, a hint, a smile. I elbowed my way through them, dragging Tally with me. Rosa followed easily in our wake, her head high, her eyes flashing danger at creatures she considered to be *peones* beneath her notice. But if we hoped they'd leave us alone, we were mistaken. They trooped down the hill behind us, shouting and scribbling on their note pads. Finally, desperate, I turned and faced them.

"Can't you leave us alone? Haven't we had enough trouble?" I sounded like a sparrow.

And then came a familiar voice. "Gentlemen! She's going on the theatrical circuit. I've got her booked from here to Kansas City. You've had Mazeppa. You've had Lotta Crabtree. Now you have Pearl Hart, the Bandit Queen, who sings like an angel."

Rosa swirled her skirts and held out her hands, while I stood frozen in place, my mouth open. "What've you done, for God's sake?" I blurted.

"Some welcome!" Dan grinned his familiar grin. "Sweetheart, we're going to get rich. I've got us space on the train to Tucson. And then to Tombstone and the Orpheum in Bisbee."

He took my arm with one hand and Rosa's with the other,

but I pulled free, looking for Tally. She stood at the edge of the platform, watching us, fear and longing plain in her eyes.

"Come on, Tally," I said. "Where I go, you go."

She was trembling. "You sure?"

"I'm sure. The three of us have to stick together."

One of her radiant smiles spilled across her face. "I'll take care of that baby when it comes. Don't you worry."

Although the unborn child had gotten us free, I still hated the idea of it. And now I had to explain to Dan why his grand tour would have to be cut short. "It's all yours," I said to Tally. "Now let's go, before the train leaves without us."

"Rosa would like that fine," she said.

Once I'd thought I loved Dan, but that had been long before, and I'd been somebody else, a woman I could hardly remember. Still, he'd cared enough about me to arrange this tour, to be at the prison gates, waiting. The question was, what did I want now? And who was I? Life had forced me into playing so many parts that, standing there in the station in Yuma, I felt like a spinning top, whirling out of control and waiting for a hand to stop me.

Suddenly I was dizzy. I took a deep breath. No one could help me but me, and Rosa was welcome to Dan, if that's what they both wanted. Taking Tally's hand, I marched toward the train and the unknown future.

Dan was bubbling over with plans and talking so fast I couldn't get a word in.

"We'll play the Bird Cage first. Tombstone's a good place for a dress rehearsal, and folks there don't get much first-class stuff these days. Then we'll hit the Orpheum in Bisbee. Pearl" — he darted a glance at me — "you'll come on and sing a lullaby for your kids so far away. That'll get 'em. It always does. Then you change into a shirt and pants and come back and sing that poem you wrote. I've got a pistol you can use.

189

Shoot a few blanks and give 'em a thrill. Then I've got a little prison number I've been working on. There won't be a dry eye in the whole damned house. How's that sound?"

"Awful," I said. "The whole thing. And that poem stinks."

"Nobody'll notice. They'll be too busy looking at you. And I'll cover up weak spots with the piano." He cocked his head. "I went to a lot of trouble booking this act, so what's eating you? You got any better ideas?"

The trouble was that, as usual, I had none. All I knew was that I couldn't go home until the baby came, and even then I'd be in disgrace with a bastard child and a black nursemaid who'd murdered her own baby in a fit of terror. How was Toledo society going to swallow that? I leaned back in the seat and looked out at the desert that had captured my heart and imagination from the first. There was the green lace of the paloverde trees, the saguaros jutting up like sturdy thumbs, and behind them, shimmering on the horizon, a forest of mountains holding up the sky.

To survive with any decency, one needed the fortitude of those mountains and the patience of a desert plant that waited for the time to bloom. There was a lesson to be learned, a taking of a kind of knowledge that had always been foreign to me. I'd spent my life running, grabbing what I thought I wanted, and disregarding the consequences — to myself and to others.

I turned away from the sun-scorched landscape and blinked as I looked into Dan's sparkling eyes. "The first thing," I said, "is that I have to leave Arizona until my prison term is up. And the next is . . . ," I hesitated, not wanting to say the words. "The next is that I'm pregnant."

His eyebrows shot up to his hairline, and his mouth opened, a red "O" in the midst of his black beard. After a minute he said wryly: "And is there anything else?"

I shook my head. "Isn't that enough?"

"Who's the happy father?"

Rosa caught my wrist before I could hit him, and I felt her anger humming in her fingers. "You damn', dumb *cabrón!*" she hissed. "You think she wanted this? You think in prison she played whore? You want to know, I'll tell you how it was. How that guard watch her day and night, drooling like a mad dog. How he drag her off and do it . . . that thing you men do best . . . and you sit there and speak to her like she's trash. You dare to make fun."

She threw my hand back into my lap, and I looked down at it, and at the slight swelling of my belly. What was it I'd been thinking about fortitude?

"Jeezuz." Dan leaned across and patted my knee. "I'm sorry. I never thought. . . ." His voice trailed off, and he looked at me perplexed. "So how you going to live? You have any money?"

"No."

He thought for a minute, humming under his breath. "O K," he announced then. "Here's what we'll do. We'll play Tombstone and Bisbee. They can't expect you to disappear out of here overnight. Then we'll go across the border. Naco. Cananea. Agua Prieta. Those places. You have a few months before. . . ." He stopped. "Before. Right?"

I nodded.

"So you need money. We'll make it. Then you go and have the kid. How's that sound?"

He looked at each of us, but it was Tally who answered. "We do what we have to," she said. "We all done it before."

Chapter Thirty-Nine

Tombstone, at the end of 1902, was not the boom town it had been only twenty years before. The mines had flooded, and this, together with a drop in the price of silver, had contributed to its slow degeneration. Yet some believed that the town was on its way back to the days of former glory. The Tombstone Consolidated Mines Company had installed pumps to pump out the water, and mining had begun again on a small scale, bringing people back to the little town on Goose Flats — miners, storekeepers, freighters joined the ranchers and Mexicans who had never left.

But on that winter day when we got out of the stage and stood looking around, it seemed to me I'd arrived at the end of the earth. Smoke from mesquite fires scented the air, and a bitter wind blew off the Dragoon Mountains and sang in my ears like a funeral dirge. Trash and tumbleweeds skittered down the dusty street and piled up against crumbling adobe walls and empty hitching posts.

"Tombstone," I muttered between chattering teeth. "An appropriate name."

"Believe me, there's worse places." Dan took my arm. "Come on. Let's get settled and then go look at the theater. It hasn't been used for a while, but I talked the mayor into letting us use it. For old time's sake."

"You're a hopeless romantic," I said, laughing.

He looked startled, then said: "Isn't everybody? Isn't that what show business is about?"

"I never thought."

"And look where it's got you." He gave a tug at my arm. "Now let's go before you catch cold and lose that pretty voice of yours."

We registered at the Arlington Hotel on Allen Street as the Sandeman Acting Troupe, but news of my arrival had gotten there before me. The clerk at the desk appraised me over the top of a pair of spectacles and smiled a welcome. "Glad to have you with us, Miss Hart," he said. "You'll draw a full house tonight."

Suddenly I was afraid, remembering the faces that had stared at me in the train, faces belonging to people who seemed to want my soul. I turned away without answering and stumbled over Dan's trunk.

Rosa caught me. "She needs to rest," she said. "*Then* we go to see this theater."

"I need to write a letter before anything," I said.

Rosa smiled grimly. "Yes. The letter. And I will mail it for you."

The three of us shared a room that had a window looking out onto the street. Outside, clouds were gathering over the mountains, and the light that shone through them was weak, old, as tired as I felt. Life on the road was obviously not all pleasure.

I sent Tally to the desk for pen, ink, and writing paper. When she came back, she was frowning.

"What?" I asked.

She put down the inkwell and stared at me. "He say . . . that man . . . that he's stretchin' the rules, lettin' me stay here. He say there's a law in town that black folks ain't allowed out after dark, and I better take care."

"That's nonsense!" I said, then remembered how Harry Hu had been treated. "What did you tell him?"

She folded her arms and looked fierce. "I say I'd go out

whenever I pleased. That I was part of the troupe. He didn't much like it."

"*Chica,* you will go with me, and I'll take care of anybody who even looks at you." Rosa had lit a lamp and, in the fragile glow, she reminded me once again of a *santo,* one of those carved saints so beloved by the Mexicans.

I picked up the pen and began my letter to Herbert Brown, naming Ed Simmons and the guard I did not know as the cause of my downfall. When I finished, I struggled to find the words for what I felt, the hopelessness of the situation in which I found myself. "We're still prisoners. Never mind that we're not behind bars. I'm stuck with a baby. Tally's an outcast because she's black, and Rosa's a Mexican. All three of us are women. We're stuck with that, too. The deck was stacked the day we were born."

Rosa brought me up short. "I, for one, am glad to be out of jail, and so should you be. Don't waste time feeling sorry for yourself. Not ever. You only shame yourself." Then she softened her words with a smile. "Take a *siesta.* Then we go see this Bird Cage *Señor* Dan thinks is so wonderful. Me, I go to mail this and light a candle in a church, if there is a church in this place."

What for?" I asked, diverted as she had no doubt intended.

"For the devil to take Simmons," she said wickedly. "What else?"

Like the rest of the town, the Bird Cage was showing its age and results of neglect. The curtains were dusty and tattered, the boards of the stage were splintered, and spider webs decorated the boxes where once, so Dan told us, gentlemen had entertained their women in privacy. But it was a theater, and I had never sung in one, or acted anywhere.

I stood on the stage, looking out at the empty benches, the

battered chairs, and fought off nerves. "Are you sure I can do this?" I asked Dan.

"Talking isn't any different from singing," he assured me. "You come out, sing the lullaby, tell about your children waiting for you to come home, wipe your eyes like you're bawling your head off, and exit. Believe me, baby, they'll be eating out of your hand when you come back on and start shooting."

I guessed he was right. It was a sentimental time, and nobody was more sentimental than a bunch of men away from home.

"Just listen to me," he went on. "I been in this business since I was born. Now get back here and try on these clothes."

In the first scene I was to wear a cape and under it, breeches, shirt, boots.

"So you can walk off and come right back without changing," he explained. "Try these pants. I guessed at your size." He tossed a pair of denim trousers at me.

Tally, who had been watching us, began unbuttoning my dress. "Those pants ain't going to fit," she said. "Lucky I can sew."

"Babies!" I wanted to throw a tantrum, to lie down on the floor and howl and pound my fists.

"Now you quit!" She put her hands on my shoulders and gave me a shake. "I can fix these in a minute. Just let me get a needle and an extra piece of something. And, besides, you can leave your shirt hang out. Folks won't know about the pants or the baby."

Sane, sensible Tally — so different from the woman I'd first known. With something to do, a contribution to make, her face shone, her needle flashed, and she hummed to herself as she sewed. From then on she was our wardrobe mistress — a title given her by a grateful Dan — along with a pile of his mending.

195

★ ★ ★ ★ ★

That night I caught a glimpse of what Tombstone had been like in its heyday. All kinds of people came to the theater — ranchers down from the hills and up from the valley, shop-keepers and their wives, miners with dirt still clinging to their clothes, and whole families of Mexicans, some of the women carrying babies. With the lamps lit and the old curtains in shadow, it was easy to think back, to feel the echoes of all those others who had been on the stage before me — minstrels and magicians, Eddie Foy, Pauline Markham and her "Pinafore on Wheels," roving thespians of all kinds. I was in fine com-pany.

Dan went on first. "To warm them up," he explained. And then Rosa in a red gown, carrying her guitar as if it were a living thing, which in her hands it was.

"Break a leg," Dan whispered to me before the curtains parted, and, when I looked at him in horror, he laughed low in his throat. "It means good luck. Now git!"

And then I was alone on stage, and the faces that watched me were the faces of everyone who'd ever been curious about Pearl Hart, but with a difference I could almost feel. It was as if I belonged to them, as if they were proud of what I'd done, and they'd boast about me later to their friends. It was as if they'd all ridden alongside that afternoon in Cane Springs Cañon, urging me on, shouting encouragement. Sentimental? Perhaps. And violent, too, longing for the thrill of the chase, the success of the underdog. And in that moment, I understood and became one of them as, indeed, I had been all along.

I sang my heart out that night as I relived my past. I sang for my children, even the one unborn, and the audience came with me, cheering, whistling, clapping, and never mind that the poetry was dreadful, and my acting stilted. When I shot off the pistol, the entire theater rose to its feet and roared.

They called me back for encores again and again, and I obliged with the songs I knew and loved until I couldn't sing any more. My performance was praised in the paper and the review was reprinted in others, and, in my moment of triumph, I forgot that I was leaving a trail anyone could follow. What mattered was success — and the money jingling in my pocket. What mattered was the glory of it all.

Chapter Forty

The road to Bisbee ran south through the San Pedro Valley. I can close my eyes and see it still, that valley spreading out, graceful and mysterious, the grass a dull gold and the mountains on either side the pale rose and faint lavender of winter. And on the horizon another mountain loomed.

Rosa pointed. "From here you can see into Mexico. That's Cananea."

How I stared! How I clutched my hands together and ignored Rosa's next words. "Why so sad, *chica?*"

What I had was a memory of a day spent with a man who had, in spite of my good intentions, turned into a fairy tale. *Once upon a time,* I told myself, *I knew a good man.* So I stared out and did not answer her, and the road rose gradually into the Mule Mountains, and Mexico was blotted out by rocks and the dark green of oak trees clinging to steep cliffs.

Up and up. It seemed we would touch the sky. And then we crested, and Bisbee lay at our feet, awake as Tombstone had been asleep, raucous, rowdy, its streets narrow cañons chiseled through red rock, its heart the richness of the copper ore mined in the tunnels that honeycombed the earth.

The Orpheum Theater stood at the foot of Brewery Gulch, where it joined Main Street. And outside it was a poster. **Miss Pearl Hart**. **Arizona's Bandit Queen**, it read.

I turned mystified to Dan. "How did that happen?"

"You're famous. And people, being what they are, have what my mother used to call 'an unhealthy curiosity.' They all want to see you, feisty little critter that you are."

Once I'd stood, listening entranced to Julia Ward Howe and Helen Modjeska, wishing to make my mark on the world. Now it seemed that I had, but it wasn't the kind I'd hoped for.

We registered at the Johnson Hotel, though I looked with longing at the newly finished Copper Queen that advertised rooms with private bath and superior dining.

"I'd kill for a tub and hot water," I said.

"Famous isn't rich. At least not yet," came the brusque answer.

"Some day," I promised myself. "Some day I'll come back. And have a fancy room. And eat in a restaurant with candles and wine and maybe music."

We walked to the theater, down streets crowded with people, horses, burros carrying water in huge bags and wood for the cooking fires of the miners' shacks that were built on the sides of the hills. The saloons and gambling houses were wide open. I heard music, voices, laughter even as I saw the whores from the cribs at the high end of the street, eyeing passers-by like hungry cats.

"We'll have a full house," Dan predicted, smiling at one of the whores as if she were a great beauty. "Tonight and tomorrow. Money in the bank, ladies. Money in the bank, or I'm damned."

As usual, he was right. The first night was a repeat of the performance in Tombstone, and at the matinee, the following afternoon, attended mostly by ladies — women in fine clothes as well as housewives and a few whores who took care to sit off to the side — I received cheers of approval and left the theater in fine spirits.

My good mood lasted through the evening performance, and I was singing as I left. The others had gone on without me, when they saw the people crowding the stage door to catch a close-up glimpse of the Bandit Queen.

"I'll come along soon," I told them. The streets were still busy, the walk to the hotel a short one.

Dan looked doubtful. "You're sure?"

I laughed. "I've been in tougher places than this."

But I'd had Huey. Or Joe. Or Harry. When I stepped out onto Brewery Gulch, I had only myself, and that wasn't enough. I'd taken only a few steps when someone grabbed my arms, twisted them behind my back, and pulled me into an alley.

Pain shot through my shoulders. I struggled as best I could and attempted to see the face of my attacker, but he held me too tightly.

"Bitch!" he said hoarsely, close to my ear. "Little, squealing bitch. You cost me my job. Now I'll fix you for good."

I knew him then by his voice.

"Let me go," I pleaded, realizing it was useless.

"I'll let you go, all right. When I'm finished with you." He tightened his grip and twisted harder.

It was at that moment that I felt the first flutter of life in my belly, faint as the wing beat of a baby bird but unmistakable, and I forgot that I hated the child, forgot fear in the suddenness of anger. No matter what, I was going to fight, to get free. I was going to save myself and the unborn baby that depended on me for its life. I took a deep breath, ready to scream. There were people moving on the street only a few feet away, people who would hear and come running. But he read my mind and clapped a filthy hand over my mouth.

"None of that," he growled, so close I could smell him — whiskey, stale sweat, and something else. Lust. I could feel his arousal, and terror returned to combine with anger. Not that. Not again.

I squirmed against him, heard him laugh low in his throat.

My arms were still pinned behind me, but my legs and feet were free. I lifted a foot and brought my sharp heel down on his toes once, twice, with all my strength. Then I kicked him in the shins.

Startled, he took his hand away from my face, and I screamed as loud as I could. He slapped my face, splitting my lip, and dragged me further back into the dark. He was panting like an animal and mumbling to himself, words I barely heard and didn't want to understand.

Then came the click of a pistol being cocked. "Let her go." The voice came from the entrance to the alley.

Simmons held me in front as a shield. "You want me, you'll have to shoot her," he said. "Or you can wait till I cut up this pretty face."

As he spoke, I felt the cold prick of a knife by my cheek. He would do it. I knew that as surely as I knew that, since he was now holding my wrists with only one hand, I had the slightest of chances. I stopped struggling and forced myself to relax, waiting for his grip to lessen. When it did, I said: "Don't cut me. Please."

"Tell your friend over there to back off," came the answer.

Without warning, I wrenched myself to the left, away from the knife and, almost, out of his grasp, giving my rescuer a clear shot.

But Simmons was quick. He shoved me toward the other man and took off into the dark warren of the gulch.

"Pearl. Are you all right?"

I shook my head to clear it. Surely I knew that voice. Surely I was dreaming. I said, "Cal?" tentatively.

He put an arm around my waist, and I saw his face and the blue eyes I remembered. "Let's get you home."

Home. I had no home. I started to laugh, a chuckle at first and then a surging that shook my whole body. Home. Simmons. Cal. The nerve-wracking business of standing on a stage like a freak in a sideshow. My life was like one of the novels I'd read so eagerly as a girl, except there was never an end, it went on and on, each chapter worse than the one before.

He pocketed his pistol and put both arms around me. "Don't cry," he said softly. "You're safe now."

But I knew I wasn't. Simmons was out there in the dark, waiting his chance. He'd find me again, maim me, kill me, have me sent back to live out my time in that cell.

I said: "I thought you were dead."

"Not a chance." He reached into a pocket and brought out a handkerchief to wipe my face. "But I thought you were. When you didn't answer my letters, I was sure something had happened."

"Something did." I swallowed another hysterical chuckle and leaned against him, storing up the feel of his body, its warmth, its masculine strength.

"I wish I'd known," he said. "I wouldn't have let you take such a risk."

"Well," I said, "you just saved me, and I can't thank you enough. How did you get here, anyhow?"

He took my arm and led me toward the lights of the Gulch. "I've been working in Cananea and came up for supplies. The first thing I saw was that poster, and I bought myself a ticket for the show. Luckily I came back to find you. Who was that guy?"

"A prison guard."

He looked down at me, concern shadowing his eyes. "Do you want to file charges?"

That would mean going to the law and revealing the fact that I was still in Arizona. I shook my head. "No. I just want to leave the territory. Have to, or they'll send me back. That was a part of my parole. They'll send all of us, and I can't go back. I won't!" I was trembling from shock and the memory of prison.

"You won't have to," he said. "I have an idea. But let's get you back to the hotel, and we'll talk about it in the morning."

"There's Rosa and Tally, too. I can't leave them. At least not Tally. She's got no place to go."

"Who's she?"

"She was in prison with me. We all helped each other, like a family."

He listened calmly, the kind of man to whom nothing came as a surprise. Then he said: "There's no reason you all can't come to Cananea, is there?"

Chapter Forty-One

"This man, he loves you."

We were at the station in Naco, waiting for Dan and Cal to come with our tickets, and Rosa was embroidering her favorite fantasy. But any chance of love between Cal and me had vanished in prison.

"Don't," I said, and turned away.

"Don't what? He finds you, saves you, and now takes all of us out of this hell, and you tell me *don't!* I tell you, marry him. Give your *niños,* all of them, a father and yourself a new name. Who will know in a year, in five years, who you were? No one."

"I'll know."

She snorted. "Forgetting is easy when you have a place to live and food in your belly. All over this country are women good at forgetting. Women who got themselves a husband, and never mind that they were whores first."

"I had a husband," I reminded her. "And, anyway, Cal hasn't asked me to marry him."

"He will," she prophesied. "And you will say yes, because you'll never find another like this one."

Talking to Rosa, listening to her unswayable logic, was like facing a swarm of bees. I lifted my hands to put them over my ears and saw, as I did, the bruises on my wrists. For a moment I went dizzy. I might have been killed, left with my face in tatters. That was the fate of a woman alone. That and an old age peopled by ghosts.

"No more. You've said enough," I told her, and turned as

Cal and Dan came toward us.

Cal was smiling that somehow shy half-smile that had touched me years before, and his eyes were as blue as a summer lake. As if in recognition, the child moved again, a gentle motion different from the night before, a turning, like a sigh. "Ready?" he asked.

I let him lead me toward the train without answering, then sat, looking out the window as we left the station on our way to Mexico. At first, he didn't notice my silence but talked as if to make up for all those undelivered letters, as if he could blot out the empty years with words and a history lesson. I let him go on, touched by his attention.

"They say Coronado came through this valley, looking for gold and the Seven Cities of Cibola. It must have been something to see. All those men in armor on horseback, all the carts and burros and flocks of sheep to feed his army."

"Did he find it? The gold?" I asked, interested in spite of myself.

"Not as much as he expected. Funny that now the copper mines are making more money than he ever dreamed of. Mexico is a rich country, if a man lives long enough to discover the wealth."

That startled me. "Will we be safe in Cananea?"

He took my hand and smoothed a finger over the bruises. "I'll make sure of that. And I doubt Simmons will follow you there."

"I'll be watching over my shoulder."

"Why you?" he asked. "Why was he after you and not Tally or Rosa?"

I wanted to tell him, to be free of secrets, lies, misunderstandings, but all I said was: "He's crazy. He hated me from the first, and there wasn't anything I could do about it."

"I see," he said, but he didn't. He'd never been in prison,

never been helpless, and at the mercy of another.

"It was hell," I said.

His hand tightened over mine. "You're a courageous woman."

"Desperate," I corrected. "There's a difference."

"Not the way I see it."

"There's some who'd argue with you." I turned away to watch the land blurring into daubs of color — tawny grass, the dark green of juniper and oak, and always the mountains pushing against the sky.

How strange it was that twice in my life I would be fleeing for safety down the same valley that had been traveled by Coronado. Everything, it seemed, was all of a piece, a giant tapestry woven together with people meeting, parting, meeting again as if pulled by a common thread. I closed my eyes as much to shut out thought as for need of sleep, and felt him move away, respecting that need.

"I'll wake you when we get there," he said, his breath warm on my cheek. And then, so low I almost didn't hear, "Sleep well, my dear."

Oddly enough, I did.

We got settled in the Sonora Hotel, and Dan went off to scout a place for a performance. Rosa and Tally wanted to gossip about Cal, but I was tired and depressed. The hotel was bleak, the town a typical raw mining town, ugly and totally lacking refinement. Although I was grateful to have been rescued, it seemed I had also been abandoned, and for no reason other than my notoriety. Cal was staying up on the hill where the mine owners lived, while I had been left behind, the criminal turned showgirl. So much for the hopes of my companions!

I lay down on the bed without even taking off my shoes.

"Let me alone. I want to sleep."

Tally pulled a cover over me. "You do it. Rosa and me'll go out and see what this town is all about."

They hadn't been gone ten minutes before I was awakened by a knock on the door.

"I've come to take you to dinner."

Cal stood there, dressed in a dark suit and tie, looking very much a man of the world.

What harm? I asked myself. The evening would be another treasure to add to my memories. But, as it turned out, that innocent acceptance was the keystone of my future.

He took me to a Mexican *cantina*, adobe-walled and warmed by a fire that flickered in a stone fireplace. The heat was welcome, for the night was cold, and he apologized as he seated me in a chair beside the hearth.

"Cananea doesn't really have a good restaurant. If it did, we'd be there. But this is an interesting place, and I hope you like it."

"I do," I said, looking around with pleasure at the tiled floor, the tin-framed mirrors on the walls that reflected the firelight. "This is lovely."

"Because you're here, it is." He smiled that quirky smile.

"Please," I said, remembering Rosa's words and hoping to stop the inevitable.

"I was only saying what I thought," came his response. "I didn't mean to upset you."

"You didn't. It's just. . . ." I hesitated. "I'm not used to flattery. In prison I got used to the opposite."

"Flattery is one thing. The truth is another." He leaned his chin on his hands and gave me a level look. "I remembered how you sang that night in Globe the whole time I was gone. And I promised myself that I'd find you again. You're a lovely woman and good company. That day we spent together gave

207

me more pleasure than I've ever had. You were so happy. I'd like to see you like that all the time. But what I want to know is what you're going to do. You can't really want to spend the rest of your life on the stage or hiding from Simmons."

I sat back and looked at my hands clenched in my lap. "As soon as I have the money, I'm going home," I lied. "It shouldn't be long. You saw the crowds in Bisbee."

"And then?"

"Then I'll live the rest of my life in peace. I've earned it."

He nodded in agreement. Then he asked: "Is there anyone waiting for you? Anybody special?"

Ah, Cal! So obvious. So honest. While out of necessity I had to be devious.

"No," I said. "There's nobody. I'll never marry again," and wished I could erase the years.

"Marry me," he said, unfazed by my determination. "Say yes, Pearl."

"I . . . I can't!" The words burst out. "Please don't ask me, because I can't."

"Why not?"

Of course, he wanted an explanation. I cast around in my mind for something believable. "I've been in prison. I'm a criminal. A bad woman. You don't want to be saddled with a wife like me. I won't let you be. You deserve better."

He reached across the table and took my hand. "I know why you did what you did, and it's over and done with. Nobody else has to know. You'll be Pearl Jameson. My wife. That's all. And you can bring your children out. I'll be good to them and to you. You know that. At least, I hope you do."

I pulled away. "It's out of the question. But I thank you with all my heart."

Any other man would have accepted that statement, but Cal wasn't just any man. He was himself and determined.

208

"What's wrong?" he asked. "Something is, but I can't help you unless I know."

When he heard, he'd hate me, and I'd be finished with the whole nasty performance. I spoke around a pain in my throat that nearly choked me and told the entire story, leaving nothing out. It was as if I were seeing it for the first time, reliving the utter humiliation, the brutality. When I was through, I buried my face in my hands, refusing to look and see my shame reflected in his eyes.

He was silent a long time. When he spoke, it was in a tone I hadn't expected, serious and deadly. "I should have killed him. And I will if I ever see him again."

"No!" I dropped my hands and read the determination on his face, in the set of his shoulders. "No! There's been enough violence. Leave it. Forget it. I'm sorry I told you. I'm sorry I ever was born. There's a curse on me and on everybody around me, so leave me alone. Let me go."

"It's not that simple when you love someone," he said.

"If you trust love, you're a fool." Bitter words but necessary, and, worse, I believed them.

"Then I am, and you're stuck with me. You can't help what happened with Simmons, but you can help what happens from here. I love you, I want to take care of you, and I will, whether you want to be pig-headed about it or not." And then he smiled, and his eyes turned to blue fire, and the wall I'd built so carefully around myself began to crumble.

"You're the one who's pig-headed," I snapped, desperate. "You don't know anything about who I am or what I've done. You're in love with some person who isn't there."

"I know you're tough, independent, and a damn' fool," he said, raising a hand to summon a waiter. "All of which I respect and admire. And now let's eat and decide where the wedding is going to be."

He hadn't even kissed me, had hardly touched me, and we'd known each other for a total of three days. How could he be so certain? How could I? But, in the heart that was beating so wildly behind its crumbling wall, I knew.

Chapter Forty-Two

It sounds romantic — like the happy ending to a novel with its twists and turns, villains and heroes. But, as the saying goes, "Truth is stranger than fiction," and the story of my life certainly proves that.

Cal was a man with his mind made up. If I hadn't agreed, he'd have dragged me to the altar, and he'd have had plenty of help. Rosa and Tally were ecstatic when they heard. Dan was horrified.

"But the show!" he blurted. "What'll we do about the show?"

"Stop thinking about yourself," I said, irritated. "The hell with the show. I'm getting married."

Rosa intervened with a seductive smile. "You and me will do the show. Here, in my country, they will love us."

"And Tally stays with me," I said. "So that's settled."

"He'd better treat you right," Dan retorted. "Otherwise he'll be sorry. You tell him I said so. And tell him I'm damn' sick of rescuing you."

Once I'd thought there was something between the two of us. And there was — a loyal friendship. I patted his arm. "I think I've grown up. I'll be fine."

"Jesus, I hope so," came his belligerent answer, accompanied by a scowl that turned into a grin. He put his arms around me. "Be happy, and keep your nose clean."

Years before I'd made a vow that no man would ever lay hands on me again — a foolish utterance made in the depths of anguish. The fact that all of my children were conceived by a rape proved the impossibility of keeping such a vow. And now, here I was, married to a man of a different caliber than the others, a man whose eyes blazed with passion of a kind I'd never known. And I was terrified. Ashamed of the swell of my belly that made me ugly in my own eyes and, I was sure, in his.

I undressed behind a screen, pulled a shapeless nightgown over my head. It had long sleeves and a high neck and was full enough to hide my condition. But he would know. Even in the dark, he would know.

"Please," I said. "Put out the light."

He did as I asked, but the moon was full. It drenched the room with its own brilliance, a light so strong that even the curtains cast a moving shadow across the floor. I stood there in that moonlight, thinking of excuses, wanting to say it had all been a mistake, that marriage, good or bad, was not for me, and that my body, such as it was, was mine.

And then Cal spoke. "Come to bed. You'll freeze out there."

I thought of my honeymoon with Frank. How he'd kissed me, touched me until I cried out — and how soon it had all turned ugly.

"I'm afraid." The words were a whisper, like the sound the curtains made, moving in the wind.

He got up then. "Don't be. I'll never hurt you, my love." He cupped my face between his hands and looked down at me for the longest time before he kissed me, softly, gently, the littlest touching, like a moth wing brushing my lips.

Did he know I'd ask for more? Did he understand the hunger in my heart, and how far I'd fallen from grace? I think he did. I think he was prepared to do nothing more than hold me through the night. But, like the Sleeping Beauty, he woke me with a kiss. I put my arms around him, felt him trembling,

212

even as I was, with the holding back of desire, and I pulled his head down, met his mouth with my own, and drowned in the sheer joy of being honest with a man whose goodness knew no boundary.

Chapter Forty-Three

One minute I was standing in the parlor of our rented house, and the next I was in bed holding a baby who looked at me out of a face that was a miniature copy of my own. He lay quite still in my arms, as if he knew we'd come through a long struggle together, and he'd given me the gift of an easy birth and knew it.

"He'll never be any trouble to you," Tally pronounced. "Not now, not when he's growed. This one was born old."

Cal and I named him Dale, and Cal was as proud of him as if he were the father. Whatever worries I had on that score were forgotten as I watched him playing with and showing off the child everyone believed was his.

It seemed my life was settled at last, and I thanked God for the fact. When we returned to the States, several months later, all went as Cal had predicted. No one questioned my identity or even appeared to recognize me as the infamous Bandit Queen. To one and all I was Mrs. Cal Jameson, a happy wife and new mother.

Lulled by this sense of secure well-being, I set about making the little house into a true home for us and for Emma and Little Joe who were arriving soon, accompanied by my mother.

My spirits were high that bright fall day. I was singing as I scrubbed the porch with Dale propped in a basket by the door. Cal had gone off to town, and Tally was in the kitchen, blacking the stove.

"Soon, soon," I crooned to myself, to the baby, to the cool and brilliant air flowing around me, and heard the baby chuckle as a migrating butterfly landed on the edge of his basket and rested there.

"Pretty," I exclaimed to him. "Pretty thing!" and then, as I turned back to my scrubbing, I noticed a man coming slowly up the road. He walked with a purpose, but something in the way he moved was furtive, as if he was being cautious and watching his back trail.

I called, "Tally," in a low voice, but got no answer and stayed crouched behind the railing in the hope that he would pass us by.

Closer he came. Closer. And with a sickening lurch of my heart I recognized him — his cruel hands, his bloated face, his demented lust. How had he found me? And what did he intend? He turned and came toward the house, and I saw he was smiling. It was a smile of pure evil, full of cunning and purpose.

"Tally," I called again, afraid to move. "Tally, for God's sake." All that came in answer was the cooing of my son from under his snug blanket.

My son! Regardless of the circumstances of his conception, Dale was mine. And Cal's. Simmons had no place in our home, our lives. I stood up, prepared to fight him, to protect what was mine and what I loved.

Seeing me, he stopped, his legs spread, that fiendish smile still on his face. "Well, well," he said. "Missus Jameson."

I said: "Get out," and my fingers curled into claws.

"A fine way to greet the kid's father." He moved closer, his eyes on Dale who was waving his hands in an attempt to catch the butterfly.

"Come any closer, I'll kill you," I said.

"Sure you will. And go back to the pen for life."

"How'd you find me?" I asked, desperate to keep him talking until I could lay hands on some kind of weapon — a stick of wood, the pistol in the chest of drawers in the bedroom,

215

if somehow I could get inside.

"You ain't exactly invisible . . . you and the nigger." He put a foot on the bottom step. "Your parole ain't up. I figured you'd go back nice and quiet for the sake of the kid."

I took a tiny step toward the door, hoping he wouldn't notice. But he was observant.

"Stand still." The tone of his voice, filled with menace and a clear purpose, was more terrifying than the sight of him. I'd be lucky to live long enough to go to prison if he had his way. And that would leave Tally and Dale alone and helpless. And Cal would come back to an empty house and carnage and never know the truth.

At the thought I went crazy. I went for his eyes, his brutal face, and fury gave me strength. He toppled back into the yard, bleeding from scratches where my nails had raked his face. I bit, kicked like a mad thing, but in the end he overpowered me with a punch in the stomach and a blow to my head that knocked me to the ground where I lay half unconscious, struggling to get up and fight again.

My hand closed around a rock — a poor weapon, but better than nothing. I took a ragged breath and swallowed hard to keep from vomiting, and all the beatings of my life flashed through my head: the horrors, the agony, the blood, and the crack of my bones.

I pushed myself up on all fours, blinking to clear my sight, and saw Tally, pistol in hand, her expression as grim as death's head before she pulled the trigger. Once. Twice. The explosions echoed off the cañon walls and in my ears.

Simmons staggered back, fell, and lay quite still in a rapidly growing puddle of his own blood. Tally held the pistol on him for a long minute. When he didn't move, she stooped and picked up Dale who had begun to whimper.

"There," she said to him. "There. Nobody's gonna hurt

you or your mama. Not while Tally's here."

I said: "Is he dead?"

"If he ain't, he will be." Her face was set.

The seriousness of what had been done struck me. Tally had killed a man to save me. But who would believe us — ex-cons, and her already a convicted murderess?

"What'll we do? What'll we say when they find out?" I was babbling. The future looked even worse than it had just minutes before.

"They won't find out 'less we tell 'em," she said, putting Dale down and walking over to Simmons. "He'd've killed us. And gone away with this child and killed him, too. You know it. I know it. Now you go hitch up the wagon."

"What for?"

"We gonna take him out in those hills and leave him. And we're gonna clean up this yard and smile when that man of yours gets back. And not say anything. Let it all be on my head. I'm the one did it, and I'm glad." Her voice softened. She laid a hand on my arm. "And if you want me to go, I'll go and leave you to live in peace. You just tell me."

She meant it, that brave little woman who had just saved our lives, and whose first concern, always, was I. She stood there, and I read loyalty in her eyes and love and a shadow of doubt, as if she feared what I'd say next.

"You can't go!" I put my arms around her. "How could you even think it?"

"You never know what folks'll take into their heads to do."

That shocked me. "Even me? Even after all we've gone through?"

She shrugged. "Even so. Sometimes trust comes hard."

She was the old Tally speaking, the girl who had learned the hard way, whose life had been crueler than mine had ever been. We stood there in the yard, outside the house that now

217

belonged to me, and I knew I'd never have a better friend, not in a lifetime, that we were bound together by our pasts, the present, and the future.

"Tally," I said, speaking around a lump in my throat, "I don't think we can get along without you. And that's the truth, so help me."

Her smile trickled across her face. "I hope you never think different. Now let's clean up this mess and get on with it. And let's never talk about it again."

We buried Ed Simmons in a prospect hole, one of thousands dug into the mountains. It was deep. A long time passed before we heard his body hit bottom.

"God rest him," Tally said.

And I said: "How could you?"

"Somebody's got to care," she answered. "It must be awful to die and have nobody mind."

We drove home slowly with Dale crowing in his basket between us. The shadows were long on the valley floor, and the beginning of a crimson sunset stained the sky to the west. Cal would be home soon. At the thought I wondered if I could ever keep what happened a secret from him. But if I told, what would he think of Tally? I looked at her, handling the reins with care.

"I won't tell," I said. "I promise."

"Honey, you could tell that man anything, and he'd understand," she answered, and then said: "But maybe it's better you don't."

Silently I agreed. I could tell about myself, but Tally's life and privacy were strictly hers.

As we crossed the creek and came into the yard, we were surrounded by a cloud of butterflies, their orange and black wings swirling like a tapestry — or a blessing. They had miles to go before they reached their resting place, a long, hard journey with many falling by the way. Was it luck that got them through, or determination?

I didn't know, simply wished them well as I climbed the steps to the porch and entered the little house, my journey's end, my home.

THE END

Author's Note

Those who remember Pearl Hart remember her as a small, quiet woman who never revealed the truth of her past by so much as a word. When she died, she took her secrets with her. The diary that she kept makes no reference to any of the events in her early life, concentrating instead on day-to-day happenings in her life with her second husband.

What may be inferred from this diary is the fact that she was well educated, intelligent, and literate, giving the lie to some newspaper accounts that spoke of her as "a low type," barely able to utter an intelligible sentence. One other fact stands out in reading about her later life in her own words. She was secure and happy at last.

That her first marriage was to a gambler named Frank Hart who abused her is true. It is also true that she ran away from him after the Chicago World's Fair, supported herself by singing, and that, following the accepted pattern of abused women, took him back and lived with him long enough to bear two children.

Pearl's place in Arizona history, however, rests on the fact that in May, 1899, she and her partner, Joe Boot, held up the Globe-Florence stage in Cane Springs Cañon and were apprehended several days later in an abandoned schoolhouse near Benson.

Pearl escaped from prison in Tucson, was re-captured in Deming, New Mexico, and was sent to Yuma Prison, *not* for robbing the stage, but for the theft of the driver's pistol. At her trial — and beforehand in newspaper interviews — she spoke eloquently for the cause of women's rights, which obviously did her no good at her trial.

Her early release from Yuma has always been shrouded in mystery, but a reliable source believes that she was, indeed, pregnant, that the child was born in Cananea, Mexico, and that, when she returned to the States, she had married a second time. The name Jameson is a pseudonym. Who the real father of the child was is not known. Typically, Pearl never spoke of it.

Ed Simmons, who appears as the father in this book, is fictional, as are Tally and Rosa, although they are based on two women, one black and one Mexican, who were imprisoned at about the same time. Harry Hu is also fictional. Pearl was cooking for miners near Globe, but that is all that is known. There were, however, many Chinese farmers and storekeepers in the area.

The little house near the wash where Pearl and Cal lived is still there, still isolated and surrounded by paloverdes and citrus trees. It appears a happy house, and, again, those who knew her remember how she sat on the porch, smoking hand-rolled cigarettes, smiling, and keeping her secrets to herself.

Ed Simmons, as stated above, did not exist as such and was never shot by anyone. It is worth mentioning here that in the Pearce, Arizona, cemetery is a tombstone bearing the name Joe Boot. Whoever he was, he kept his secrets, too.

About the Author

Born and raised near Pittsburgh, Pennsylvania, Jane Candia Coleman majored in creative writing at the University of Pittsburgh but stopped writing after graduation in 1960 because she knew she "hadn't lived enough, thought enough, to write anything of interest." Her life changed dramatically when she abandoned the East for the West in 1986, and her creativity came truly into its own. THE VOICES OF DOVES (1988) was written soon after she moved to Tucson. It was followed by a book of poetry, NO ROOF BUT SKY (1990), and by a truly remarkable short story collection that amply repays reading and re-reading, STORIES FROM MESA COUNTRY (1991). Her short story, "Lou" in *Louis L'Amour Western Magazine* (3/94), won the Golden Spur Award from the Western Writers of America as did her later short story, "Are You Coming Back, Phin Montana?" in *Louis L'Amour Magazine* (1/96). She has also won three Western Heritage Awards from the National Cowboy Hall of Fame. DOC HOLLIDAY'S WOMAN (1995) was her first novel and one of vivid and extraordinary power. The highly acclaimed MOVING ON: STORIES OF THE WEST was her first **Five Star Western**, and it contains her two Golden Spur award-winning stories. It can be said that a story by Jane Candia Coleman embodies the essence of what is finest in the Western story, intimations of hope, vulnerability, and courage, while she plummets to the depths of her characters, conjuring moods and imagery with the consummate artistry of an accomplished poet. THE O'KEEFE EMPIRE will be her next **Five Star Western**.